By T.H. Cini

Cover designed by, Ivory Garlock

V:4

Copyright © 2023 T.H. Cini

All rights reserved. No part of this publication may be reproduced, distributed, or transmitted in any form or by any means, including photocopying, recording, or other electronic or mechanical methods, without the prior written permission of the publisher, except in the case of brief quotations embodied in critical reviews and certain other noncommercial uses permitted by copyright law.

ISBN: 9798396150263 (Paperback)

For my brothers, John and David

By T.H. Cini

Chapter 1: Host Road

Thursday, August 19, 1982 – 7:20 am

I woke from an incredibly unsettling dream. What alarmed me was that I had that same dream a month prior, during a heat wave in July. In that dream, I vividly remembered the sensation of sitting up in bed, the chill of the air causing me to rub my arms, and the urge to grab a jacket before leaving the house. I continued along the desolate street I lived on -- there wasn't a soul in sight. It was strange how the farther I moved through the empty streets, the colder it became. The briskness seemed to seep into my bones in the deserted night. But what was more unsettling was the strange mission I was on in that dream. It had almost seemed clear to me that I had a calling of some sort. I was to deliver a mysterious bundle that was tucked within a sack that inexplicably found its place on my back. My hands gripped the ends of the sack to relieve the weight from my shoulders, all while hunched forward to keep my balance steady; the effort was straining and it wore me out. As the dream progressed, I found myself on an incline and I was trekking up a hill. I could feel my body temperature heat up from all the effort it took me. It had burned up so much energy, that I was sweating profusely. That's when I jolted awake, drenched in sweat, my sheets clinging to me, my heart racing as I frantically tried to make sense of it all. It felt like I was caught up in some dark mission, but what that task entailed, I wasn't sure. That was the dream I had in July.

The dream I woke from that morning was similar, except this time, instead of beginning in my bed, I found myself already laboring up the hill. When I reached the summit, the skies had darkened with approaching thunderclouds. I continued along that unlit road, following others who were far ahead of me and headed in the same direction. They too had heavy loads on their backs. *What did it all mean?*

"Strange," I muttered to myself.

5:20 pm

I'd moved to Hastings from the Toronto suburbs in June of 1982. Needless to say, it was a big change to be two hours away from the city, settling into a small town with a population of barely twelve hundred.

I bought a historic two-story red brick house on Bridge Street, just a short walk from downtown Hastings. Most of the other houses along my street were century homes too. The house across from mine was also a brick century home but it was yellow instead; it seemed to be a favorite spot for pigeons to perch themselves on.

Being an avid cyclist, I took advantage of the summer weather to ride my bike along the paved streets through the countryside just outside of town. That day, I decided to switch from my road bike to my mountain bike as I wanted to try some off-roading before the season changed. I started the journey from my house continuing north passing St George's church on the right and then over the bridge that crossed over the Trent River. On the bridge were six men on the east side, with their fishing poles hung over the rail. I could hear the roaring sound the waterfalls made as I sped over the bridge. The dam was situated to the west of it. I then passed the pub before arriving at the four corners of town, where Bridge Street met Front Street. I turned west on Front Street, which, after a bend, morphed into River Road. Directly after the bend was a large hill that tested my endurance early on the ride. Once over the hill's crest, the passageway was very pretty, allowing me to view the Trent River as I peddled by. That's when I heard the familiar border collie's bark followed by the rustling of grass.

"Give it a break, ya mutt," I grunted.

Almost every day that dog would chase me along the fence in its yard, stopping once it reached its boundary. It scared the shit out of me at first, but I got used to it. I still found it annoying.

Along the river was a gravel path lined with young maple and sumac trees situated on the grass lane next to the water's edge. There were too many pedestrians on the gravel path, so I chose to ride along the road. I carried on River Road for another half-mile before reaching the trailer park and then turning onto Asphodel 6th line. There I enjoyed the scenery, consisting of a large well-kept chicken farm, a dairy farm, and soya fields. It was paved, which made the ride incredibly smooth.

I continued pushing hard for a mile or two, then decided to turn back to River Road, where I continued further westward with the intention of exploring a more rugged route. I continued pedaling along for another hundred yards, moving to the middle of the road to avoid some overhanging trees that obstructed my view. I discovered nothing but late summer weeds and tall grass along the ditch, so I turned back. Moments later, I noticed a dirt lane hidden by the trees protruding onto the roadway. Upon a closer view, I discovered a road sign at the end of it called *Host Road*. It seemed hidden from plain sight, and only those who hiked or cycled would have had the opportunity to come across it. Those driving by would certainly miss it. The strangeness of my discovery piqued my interest to the point that I decided I needed to explore it further.

While sitting still on my bike, I studied the long dirt lane. It appeared to be a dead-end road that led to what seemed like an old house. The road was certainly no longer maintained by the municipality, as it had two large pathways dotted with depressions. It seemed as though it hadn't been driven on in some time; it was overgrown with tall grass and prickle bushes that leaned inward along the brown and rocky tracks. The road was perfect for a mountain bike trail.

"What do you think, Jimmy? Should we give it a try?" I muttered to myself, before steering my front tire onto one of the tire paths, a sense of anticipation tingling through me. *Here goes nothing*.

As I carried on along the road, to my right and facing east I enjoyed the view of the tall umbrella-shaped maple trees, even though they didn't shade me from the sweltering afternoon sun from the west. Past the maple trees was a wooden fence where four Holstein cows grazed a hundred or so yards away. To my left, the tall grass blew gracefully in the breeze. I continued along the road until I came to a gravel driveway of what appeared to be an abandoned farmhouse. On the rusted metal mailbox was painted "Host," its letters uneven and poorly angled. The grass along the side of the house stood at least a foot tall, a tangled mess of gnarly weeds weaving through it. Despite the neglect, the wooden steps leading to the front door remained surprisingly sturdy and intact.

Curiosity got the better of me, so I laid the bike on the driveway and made careful steps to the old house that still appeared sturdy, as the mortar between its red bricks was still robust. Some of the four-panel windows were broken and the screen door to the front entrance was pulled down and away from the frame, hanging on by two of the three hinges. I maneuvered in front. The wooden door behind it was closed shut, but I still felt the need to knock before entering.

I waited at least a minute but I jumped at the sound of a cow's bell clanking far off in the field. I knocked once more, then timidly turned the knob and it creaked when I twisted it. I pushed the door open. And directly in front was the main staircase. To my left, was a run-down-looking living room. Dust particles hung in the air, presented by the sunbeam that shone from one end of the staircase to the living room. I was taken aback by the musty, moldy odor. Once in, I discovered a large hole in the center of the living room ceiling where plaster hung down, resembling an inverted volcano. Before moving any further, I hesitated. *Is this place even safe? Maybe I should just turn back.* I reached for the door handle, but then I hesitated.

"Maybe just a little tour..."

I stepped on a creaky step towards the living room when I noticed another doorway to the left which, when I entered, determined it to be the kitchen. It was still fully furnished with an electric stove and a large industrial-sized fridge made by Viking. The table was pale green with ribbed chrome corners and three chairs, two of which were pushed over; the one remaining upright had several holes, its padding spilling out like puss from a ruptured pimple. The décor was from the late 1960s or early 1970s. I couldn't really tell which. When I peeked through the slats of the horizontal blinds, I heard a low rumble, which caused me to jump and look out at the living room, thinking the noise was coming from the house. It wasn't, so I made quick pace to the front door coming to the conclusion that it was thunder.

I closed the wooden door and peered up at the dark clouds forming. I raced home before I got caught in the downpour.

Friday, August 20, 1982 -- 5:20 pm

"Well? What do you think, Jimmy?" I asked myself while driving my 1979 green Saab 900 home from work. "Shall we head out to the pub for a pint and get take-out tonight?" I said to myself in thought. I talked to myself every once in a while. Actually, I had more so in the last year. It seemed that the greater the stress became for me, the more I talked to myself.

Although I usually would have wanted to ride my bike and get some fresh air after work, the thought of sipping a pint and not having to worry about what to make for dinner was sort of a treat for me at the end of the week. So, to the pub I went to.

* * *

"You gonna have another pint there, Jimmy?" said Big Al the bartender, his deep voice resonating through the bar.

I spied my pint glass, which was nearly empty. "Yeah, sure. And a pound of medium wings to go."

I gulped the remainder of what was left in my glass, anticipating the full pint Big Al was going to send my way when I felt a tap on my shoulder. I swung around to view a man of about sixty with leathery-tanned skin and yellowish-gray wiry hair. He had a rather large pointed nose on a small face. He was tall and thin with stained clothes. The man had a longish neck and his large Adam's apple protruded from it. He bore a slight hunch while he stood in front of me.

"Hey, pal," the man said. "Can you spare a cigarette?" His jittery eyes flashed between me and the patron sitting beside me. I was so annoyed by the disturbance that I could feel the muscles on my face tense.

"Buzz off, man! I'm trying to relax." I sneered and turned away.

He backed off, "OK. OK." He turned to the patron beside me. "How about you, pal?"

I glanced sideways at the exchange.

"No, man. I told you before, I don't smoke," the man replied with a huff. "Here." He shoved his hand in his pocket, fished out a two-dollar bill, and held it out in front of the beggar.

"Buy yourself some."

The scraggly-looking man leaned over and gracefully took the crumpled banknote. "OK. OK. Thank you," he grunted, backing away from us, bowing as he did. He eventually left in a hobble.

"I wouldn't have given him a thing," I snarled, my lip curling in disdain as I whipped around to face Big Al. They called him "Big Al" as he was a tall man—well over six feet with a large frame. He had a rather imposing figure. He was middle-aged, bald, and sported a short, thick mustache. Before speaking, the barman spread out his arms and placed them on the bar surface; it was a sort of commanding stance. Even though the size of his body was intimidating, he had a glimmer of kindness in his eyes.

"Don't be so hard on Freddie," the barmen said in a low gruff voice. "He's harmless. He's had a rough life," he explained.

I avoided the unpleasant glare, not understanding Big Al's reasoning for defending him. My fellow patron smirked as he slid off his stool and waved, "Night gents."

I'd seen that "Fred" before. It wasn't uncommon to spot him roaming the streets, clutching a Styrofoam cup of coffee, muttering to himself, or pestering passersby for cigarettes. For some reason, it grated on me. Maybe it was because I thought it made this quaint little town seem dirty. I left the city to avoid creatures like Fred, or so I thought. *There's no use for people like him in this town, is there, Jimmy?* I said to myself.

* * *

When I made the decision in March of that year to move to a rural town, my friends back in the suburbs made it clear that they would visit; although none of them had up to that point. There was also Susan, a woman I started dating in April of that year. I liked her a lot, but something changed shortly after I moved. It seemed that the only time we spent together was when I made the journey into the city. Otherwise, she was non-committal to any plan that involved her coming to see me in Hastings. Before opening the box of chicken wings I had ordered at the bar earlier, I peered over at the phone and thought to myself, *I wonder why she hasn't called*? For the first time in two months, I had to admit I was feeling kind of lonely.

Wednesday, August 25, 1982 -- 5:45 pm

It was another warm day. When I finally arrived home from work, I hurried to change into my cycling gear to ensure I would get a full ride in before it rained again; it had come down heavily for the entire thirty-minute drive home on my way from work. Once I was out on my bike, I stopped at the traffic lights at the four corners of the small town. I glanced up at the clouds hovering over me, but it didn't seem like it was going to rain again. I was relieved, but the air was thick with humidity. As I escaped town and made my way onto River Road, the hot pavement gave way to a steamy mist that hovered just above the surface. Patches of fog lay in the fields as I zoomed by—the ambiance was surreal. I continued along River Road, the tiny particles of mist moistened my face, arms, and lower legs. It seemed to provide temporary relief on an otherwise sticky day.

Every time I rode my bike it allowed me to clear my head of my workday's earlier stress and aggravation. It was something I looked forward to. After work, I was content to not have to interact with anyone and I relished in the quiet moments since my relocation to Hastings. I had embraced the bliss of being alone. Yes, solitude had become my sanctuary, my personal utopia.

Continuing along on the hazy road I witnessed a tall object coming towards me. I was startled at first; the rhythm of its movements was steady. The clip-clop sound is what I recognized first. *Oh! It's a woman riding a horse.* Upon closer view, the woman appeared to be a little older than I initially thought, but her blue eyes sparkled, paired with lines that formed when she smiled. She reminded me of Susan, the woman I had been dating. As she trotted by, her lovely shoulder-length brown hair bounced with the rhythm of the horse's clip-clop. She nodded gracefully as she passed. I returned the gesture. Moments later I needed to maneuver the bike to avoid a large pile of horse manure, which produced warm steam that rose, blending in with the already present curtain of fog.

I had gained a pretty good speed passing Asphodel 6th line and then missing the entrance to Host Road. I once again had to circle back, discovering the steamy mist lifting high above the hot pavement that was rising about five feet. As I approached the entrance to the dirt road, a misty tendril curled upwards and it transformed into a shape resembling a hand. With eerie fluidity, it contorted into a finger-like gesture, beckoning me towards the path before evaporating. The surreal movements halted me and I shook my head in disbelief.

"What... What the hell was that?" I exclaimed breathily.

Too many times in my youth, I turned down a dare. In my teen years and even in adulthood, I was too nervous to take chances on life. My friends used to taunt me for it, but I didn't care. Something about that felt different. It was unlike me, but I took the chance. I pushed off and carried on through one of the tire paths of the neglected road, splashing through the odd puddle until I reached the farmhouse. I stopped for a moment, leaned my left foot on the gravel, while my right rested on its pedal. I studied the aged, structure for a moment before turning my attention to the sound of cars speeding along the road in the distance. I pushed off with my left and lowered my gear so that I could maneuver through the uneven grassy landscape until I made my way to a ridge overlooking County Road 2, the same road I would take home. The cliff was about thirty feet high; a long patch of grass angled steeply downward to the pavement. I watched the cars race by on the damp pavement.

I rested on the edge of the overhang for a few minutes then turned with the intention of taking Host Road to River Road and then home, but the farmhouse drew me to it once again. I continued towards it, dropping my bike to the gravel and placing my running shoe on the first wooden step before entering. Once in, I took in the commanding staircase; its hand banister handsomely sculptured. I took the first step, which creaked loudly beneath my weight, prompting me to pause and listen. Nothing resonated from the floor above so I continued, making careful steps up and feeling for any loose boards before putting my full weight on each. I felt an unusual pressure as I ascended mid-way up the staircase; it was as if my body temperature had just increased and my heart was fluttering in my ribcage like a butterfly. I slowly continued, gradually to the top.

"Whoa!" I exclaimed loudly with a hand flying to my forehead.

Once at the top of the staircase, I took in the layout of the second floor. Directly in front of the landing was a hallway, the hardwood floor had caved in directly above where the plaster had broken through the living room below. The hallway led to rooms left and right, but I was captivated by the room directly across from the landing. The bedroom was dull and drab with a hot water radiator under the window. Something about what lay beyond the bedroom window struck my attention and prompted me to navigate around the busted floor to reach the particular window. There, I saw that it was raining. It was a west-facing window, displaying County Road # 2, cars splashing along it through the downpour.

"Huh? The road wasn't soaked like this just a minute ago."

I quickly retraced my steps across the hallway, down the stairs and out the front door to discover a thick fog, but no rain. I nearly cursed to myself, "What in the . . ."

I raced back upstairs again, but this time I required the assistance of the top post of the banister to steady myself from the sudden onset of dizziness. I huffed out, "Woah there!" I took a few breaths, blinking quickly as I felt as if I was going to pass out.

What the hell, Jimmy? Did you even have enough to eat before you took off on the bike? You need to grab a bite to eat next time.

After a few moments, and feeling stable once again, I let go of the rail, stepped around the broken floor and into the sparse bedroom to stand directly in front of the window. *It's raining!* It was dark and even the window was covered with raindrops.

"What's going on, Jimmy?" I asked. "Are you losing your mind?"

I continued staring out of that mystifying bedroom window, watching car after car splash by. That's when I saw it, a car identical to mine driving through the rain.

Wait a minute... I thought I was the only one who had a green Saab 900 in the area. And that dent on the front fender... Is it in the same place as mine? No, No, that's not right. It couldn't be...

I rushed down the stairs to view the low mist hovering just above the grassy field; the rhythmic call of the frogs could be heard from the river bank in the distance -- but there was no rain. When I glanced up at the house I felt shivers, so I reached for my bike and rode along the road until arriving at River Road, where the pavement was virtually dry. *Something very strange is going on in that house!*

6:45 pm
Once I set my bike in the basement and locked the front door, I scanned my watch which read just before 5:40 pm.

"What?" I glanced from my watch to the closest window, "Can't be that early. It's gotta be later than that."

I paced to the kitchen where the clock read 6:45. To further confirm, I checked the living room clock which also read the same.

"Damn! I liked this watch too," I removed it from my wrist and placed it to my ear. I listened to the ticking of the automatic movement. "It's running all right. I guess it's just running slow." I shrugged my shoulders, glancing at the watch again. I reset the time, fitted it over my wrist, and then went about preparing dinner.

Thursday, August 26, 1982 – 6:20 pm
Yesterday's prior events ran through my mind, specifically the view from that bedroom window. It was abnormal. I knew it wasn't in line with anything else I'd experienced before. To be honest, I was fearful *and* intrigued. Just the thought of it caused my chest to tighten and my skin prickle. But I needed to re-enter that upstairs bedroom once again, so off I went to that old farmhouse on Host Road.

There I was peering up from the bottom of the staircase, placing my foot on the first step. As I ascended the staircase, I could feel my blood pressure shifting, mirroring that first day's sensation, therefore; I needed to proceed cautiously and take each step deliberately. I kept one hand on the railing for stability in case I felt a pang of dizziness hit me like the day prior.

At the top of the staircase, I navigated past the hallway hole to the empty bedroom and finally to that curious window where I was the day before. As I looked outside, the weather and sky remained unchanged from the moment I stepped into the house: the weather was mild, with an overcast sky casting a soft, diffused light over the landscape. It mirrored that all day, so nothing seemed out of the ordinary.

I continued peering out into the gray, dank surroundings, watching car after car breeze by. I was beginning to lose hope when I looked at my watch. It read 5:15 pm.

"What?" I shook my wrist, then pressed the watch to my ear. "It's working," I confirmed to myself and continued staring out the window.

I shook my head and squinted my eyes as I spoke to myself, "Something strange is going on."

I'm not sure if I was anticipating something extraordinary to happen, and honestly, I found myself hoping for it. Yet as I stood there, waiting with bated breath, nothing happened. Disappointment washed over me like a wave, leaving me deflated.

Well, Jimmy. I guess you were just seeing things yesterday. Maybe you need to be—.

Just as I was going to finish rambling on in my head, I saw that green Saab 900 again – with the same dent as mine. But not just that, there was something else. The man inside the Saab was wearing a coral blue shirt. *I was wearing a coral blue shirt today!* I usually drove along that part of County Road 2 around 5:15-ish, but that was an hour ago! *Was that . . . it couldn't be. Something strange is going on, really strange.*

Chapter 2: The One Hour and Seven Minute Delay

Friday, August 27, 1982 -- 5:20 pm
After work that day, I decided I wanted to test something out. I borrowed a reflective striped vest from my workplace and set it on the passenger side of the dashboard before leaving work. I then took my usual route home, but when I approached the cliff on County Road 2, I struggled to locate the farmhouse from that vantage point causing me to slow my vehicle to have a better look. The car behind me honked, so I downshifted, hit the gas, and sped home.

5:50 pm
I ate a half slice of bread that was loaded with peanut butter for some energy, and off I went through town on my mountain bike. I'd finally become familiar with the trees that jut out and obstructed the pathway that initially obscured my view of Host Road. I turned onto the dirt path and cycled down. The afternoon sun was still warm, even though it had lowered on the horizon. I labored along the dirt road until I reached the gravel driveway where I dropped the bike. Before I entered the house, I checked my watch and it read 6:25 pm. I opened the door and entered the musty house. I made evenly timed steps up the staircase to ease onto the second floor and relieve myself from not getting a dizzy spell. Once at the top of the staircase, I took a minute to catch my breath and maintain my balance because I still felt uneasy on my feet.

I paced towards the strange window and checked my watch: 5:20 pm. There! It happened again. I let out a heaved sigh. *My watch is once again over an hour behind!* I waited by the window for another ten minutes, gazing out at the road while the late afternoon sun was glowing. The golden rays reflected off of the glass and shone into my eyes. I squinted, casting my gaze from outside the window and then towards my watch. I was stuck in my thoughts, trying to concentrate on each car that flew by. I clenched my jaw tight and crossed my arms with impatience.

Jesus Christ, Jimmy! Why didn't you see the damn house? What is wrong with you... Are you blind?! It couldn't be that hard. And why the hell did you speed up? It probably didn't even give me enough — that's when I saw it! I saw me, yes, me, in my 1979 green Saab 900 with the reflective vest on the dashboard. I watched as I slowed the car, and got honked at before accelerating.

"What in the hell . . ." I brought my hand to my head as I turned away from the window. "What's going on here?"

I turned and pressed my back against the plaster wall, sliding to the floor, staring out at the staircase, taking in the strangeness of what I just witnessed. Beads of sweat collected on my forehead and I glanced down at my watch.

"Wait a minute... I'm an hour behind! That's it! I'm technically in the past by an hour. How can that be?"

I closed my eyes and took in a few deep breaths as that odd phenomenon sank in. *I need to get home. I need to see what the real time is.*

6:47 pm
After placing my bike in the basement, I hurried upstairs and checked both clocks. They read 6:47 pm and my watch read exactly 5:40 pm.

OK, so if I have this right...That room in the farmhouse puts me exactly one hour and seven minutes behind. This is ludicrous!

Sunday, August 29, 1982 -- 3:05 pm
It was finally the weekend so I had some time to experiment with the one-hour and seven-minute delay I experienced two days before; so, I parked my car alongside the grass cliff that I viewed from the house window. I placed my four-way flashers on and climbed the steep embankment. I angled the soles and heels of my shoes inwards to dig deep into the turf, but every once in a while I lost my balance and slipped on the grass as I continued to the crest of the escarpment. Once I was up, I flattened my hand against my forehead to shield my eyes from the bright afternoon sun. *Where's the farmhouse?* I questioned myself, as my body screwed from the left and right. *I don't see it!* I checked my watch. It read 3:08 pm. *I only got ten minutes before I should get home and hop on the bike.*

The tall grass was thick and caught on my shoe every time I lifted my foot to make a step forward. It took much effort. I continued for five minutes or so until I reached a fence that surrounded the field of Holsteins that I'd seen on my bike ride a few days prior. *So, if the cows are here...* I turned around . . . *then the house should be right about there*. I pointed West with my index finger. *But there's... no house?* Not only was there no house, there was no dirt road either. My jaw clenched as I was stuck in thought. Confusion swirled in my mind as I tried to make sense of what was going on. I checked my watch once again, which read 3:19 pm. *I'd better head back to ensure I'm in line with my rediscovery in an hour and seven minutes.* I trudged onto the cliff's edge and angled myself down the steep slope, occasionally slipping until finally beside my Saab.

4:00 pm
I made it home, quickly changed into cyclist attire, ate a poorly toasted peanut butter sandwich, and off I went through town and along River Road like I had the past few days.

I scanned my watch while pedaling before turning on Host Road. *We've got ten minutes, Jimmy.* The grass brushed against my wheels and spokes as I zoomed through the right dirt path until in front of the house. I dumped my bike on the gravel and entered the house. I took one long breath in, released it slowly, and crept up each step. As I took mindful steps up the staircase, I braced myself for the change in blood pressure, which was evident mid-way up. I paused, took another breath, and continued. I steadied myself after each of the last eight steps, grappling with my heavy breaths and sweat perspiring on my forehead. I took a glance at my watch, which read 3:11 pm; it was already at least forty minutes behind. Once I was up the stairs completely, I exhaled and waited a moment before continuing across the hallway to the bedroom window. I peered out to view the lumpy mounds of grass that continued to the cliff. My watch read 3:06 pm but it was supposed to be around 4:15 pm.

There! I let out an excited huff through my nostrils. My eyes widened as I saw myself. Me! *That's me parking my car with the flashers blinking.*

Seconds later, I watched myself exiting the car. *It's me. This is... Surreal... This is unlike anything I've ever seen before!*

I studied myself as I was approaching the cliff, disappearing from behind it briefly before the top of my head re-emerged. I continued watching as my other self struggled to maintain footing until finally making it to the top of the cliff, bringing my hand to my forehead.

"I'm here!" I howled out to my other self, banging on the window till it shook. "Hey! Look over here! Jimmy, it's me!"

The one-hour-and-seven-minute delay of me didn't hear

my bangs. My earlier self just wandered until I disappeared from view.

"Dammit!" I cursed and smacked the window with a flat palm. I sniffed angrily, unsure of what to do. I gripped at my hair, looking around till I saw the staircase. I jockeyed towards it and trampled down the stairs, and out the door as quickly as I could to see nothing but the tall grass blowing in the breeze.

I rubbed the side of my face in a feeble attempt to soothe my anxiety. The sweat leaked down my cheeks against the palm of my hand. "I would have been about there . . . yeah. Right there . . . and then I . . ." I cleared my throat and my Adam's apple bobbed.

I twisted myself and bolted up towards the stairs so fast that by the time I reached the top, the corridor was spinning rapidly. The only way I found the top staircase post was with the back of my head when I fell onto it and collapsed to the floor.

* * *

When my consciousness came back a buzzing fly sped past my ear, circling several times before landing on my nose. The fly buzzed away as I shifted to my knees. After a few minutes, I pushed myself to my feet and shuffled towards the window to discover that my green Saab was gone. My eyes widened.

"Shit!" I groaned and my head tipped back.

I then made careful steps down the staircase until I was out into the warm afternoon sun, its light was almost blinding as it fluttered above the horizon. That's when I came to the realization that something was missing.

"Where the hell's my bike?" I searched frantically around the house, even though I knew I left it on the gravel driveway. "It was right . . ." I pointed to the spot where I was certain I'd laid it, which was beside the mailbox. I brought my hand to my head and they both felt numb.

"That's... odd." I rubbed my fingers together a few times then continued searching, but stopped upon hearing a noise coming from down the end of Host Road; it was the crunch of twigs and the faint squeak of a wheel. When I whipped my head around and focused, I viewed a man on a bike heading my way.

"Is that . . ." I squinted my eyes, "is that who I think it is?" I backed away with a palm to my chest, turned to the house, re-entered, and slammed the door behind me. "It can't be." I shook my head in disbelief.

I looked towards the staircase again and began walking towards it. I took each step upwards, steadily but not quickly. What was strange was that I didn't feel the usual flushing hot sensation rush to my head, and was able to maintain my strength once up top. I stood still atop of the landing, listening. I heard the crash of a bike on the gravel outside the door so I darted to the bedroom window where I fell to the floor from exhaustion, resting my back against the radiator. I remained facing the staircase. A moment later I heard a crack from the front door opening, followed by shuffling that stopped for a moment, before hearing the creak of a foot pressed onto the first step of the staircase. The slow squeaks of each step were perfectly paced, simulating that of a slow-moving metronome, evenly paced . . . *squeak. . . crack . . . snap. . .*, until a shadow crept against the side wall. With no energy left to move, all I could do was squirm my rump and rapidly move my eyes, readying myself for what was to come.

The steps were steady and so was the figure that followed the shadow and finally, there I was. Me in the flesh! It was my delayed self, finally catching up.

"You," I huffed out with all the strength I had, languidly lifting my hand and pointing to my other self, as he stood atop the staircase.

"I . . ." he hesitated. He attempted to speak but seemed to struggle; his lips became limp, uneven, and wet with drool before reaching for his forehead. His eyes rolled back and he fell against the top post, crashing onto the floor beside the hole in the hallway.

"Hey!" I screamed out, pushing myself off the floor with a grunt.

"Are you OK?" I leaned over the motionless body. "Jimmy. Are you OK?"

Jimmy's chest moved up and down indicating he was still alive; his eyes remained closed. This continued for some time before he groaned and reached around to feel behind his head before opening his eyes.

He moaned in agony. "Ow! That hurts." He wobbled and struggled to his knees, grimacing. He then stared in my direction. "Oh, my God." He paused in evident shock before continuing. He slapped his face a few times then ran his fingers through his hair. "It worked. And I have a voice. I can be heard." He said before standing.

I moved up as well.

"Finally! We're apart." He scanned me up and down, pointing at me before chuckling. "You're disappearing."

I looked down at my legs, watching them morph into a translucent form, flickering in and out of sight. Panic surged within me. "What's going on?"

A sinister smirk twisted across his lips, "I can tell you what's happening. You're becoming bodiless. I'm finally rid of you!"

Chapter 3: Jimmy's Soulless Body

Sunday, August 29, 1982 -- 5:00 pm

While Jimmy's body stood there, observing the dissociation take place between this body and soul, he reflected upon how this situation came to be, specifically the year building up to it. He was well aware of being talked to by his soul, though it was more like being talked *at*. He always knew there was a bond between his body and his soul; however, his soul wasn't aware of a connection at all and therefore never acknowledged that they could ever be separated. All the time Jimmy's soul thought he was talking to himself, he never accepted the fact that they were a union, a team, conjoined since birth.

Jimmy's body didn't discover the amalgamation until they— "they" meaning his body and soul—had turned thirty. That was a little over a year ago; that's when that voice in his head—in turn, his soul—started speaking to him. Jimmy's body wasn't certain if other souls talked to themselves, but the constant chatter allowed him to become more aware of his own existence. It was sort of an awakening.

The relationship was pleasant... at first. Jimmy enjoyed the partnership that it gave him. The chatter was congenial and was like any relationship where one looked after the other. Simple comments like 'Well, that was a great day today, wasn't it Jimmy?' were common from Jimmy's soul. They were supportive and constructive, much like any well-balanced relationship would work. At the time, Jimmy's body was relaxed and limber. Sadly, the peace didn't stick around. As time passed, Jimmy's body noticed a shift. His other half grew restless, casting aside morals and connections with loved ones and left behind fractured relationships with family and friends. Selfishness took hold, bringing a wave of stress and anxiety. With the tension came a surge in internal dialogue, straining the bond between body and soul even further. It began to break down. And with that, came the self-degrading criticism: "What the hell did you do that for, Jimmy?"— the comments were snarky and condescending. That's when Jimmy's body grew resentful of his soul. It rebelled in every way it knew how, sending out distress signals through aches, tension, and nervous twitches. It even resorted to unleashing a sudden bout of diarrhea. Jimmy hoped his soul would get the message and start treating his body with more respect, but it didn't.

Despite Jimmy's head still throbbing from the fall, a sense of liberation washed over him as he realized his soul was gone. It was a strange feeling, but one he quickly embraced.

"What?" the translucent soul echoed.

Jimmy's former soul was now a ghost-like translucent image of its departed self.

Jimmy echoed back to him. "I said I don't have to listen to your voice in my head anymore," He retorted, a smirk playing on his lips.

Jimmy placed his hand on the top post and took careful steps, one by one down the staircase.

"Where are you going?" Jimmy's soul asked, still hovering at the top of the staircase.

"I'm going home."

The soul's now almost invisible entity flowed down the stairs almost bumping into its former conjoined body. He had difficulty maneuvering in his state.

"What's happening to me?"

"I don't know." Jimmy stopped and leaned in to view the see-through image, squinting before he spoke. "All I know is, you're no longer part of me." He smirked and rubbed his head. "And I'm happy to finally be rid of you." Pulling the door open, he stepped outside and mounted his bike.

"What?" his soul said, its ethereal form drifting behind his former human figure. "Wait. I'm going with you . . . right?"

"No. I'm going home to put an icepack on my head," he replied firmly, his voice strained with the effort of keeping his emotions in check.

"You can't just . . . take off on me," the soul protested.

With a swift push from his left foot, Jimmy sped down Host Road, leaving his soul trailing behind.

He carried on down the bumpy road, turning onto River Road, leaving his soul behind. The plan worked for Jimmy. He knew that strange room in that old farmhouse had some type of power. The bang on the back of his head was the perfect opportunity to expel that awful soul that had inhabited his body.

As a fresh breeze blew, he couldn't wipe the smile from his face. He was free – free of the burden of that voice barking at him from within. The tightness in his chest was suddenly gone, the tension in his neck and shoulders – vanished!

"Oh, my God. This feels so great," he expressed happily aloud.

He cycled from River Road to Front Street and then onto Bridge Street, where he stopped, got off his bike, leaned his body against the railing of the bridge and enjoyed the view of the river dam and the tiny particles of water that blessed his sun-soaked face. He closed his eyes and basked in it, taking in the rays.

Although free of a soul, Jimmy could still function as a body, his senses were alive with the sensations his new existence offered. He savored the warm breeze against his skin, relished the crisp air filling his lungs, and even found a strange comfort in the chill of the cold steel railing beneath his fingertips. With each passing moment, he embraced the freedom of his clean slate, allowing himself to laugh and smile without reservation, as if experiencing the world anew with the wonder of a newborn.

"I've never felt like this before. It's so refreshing," Jimmy remarked with a sigh. "That voice in my head never let me feel this way. It never let me just... take time and enjoy life." When Jimmy opened his eyes, he marveled at the dam's engineering, studying how it held the water's force.

He also did something he'd never done before; he just stood still, taking in life's simple pleasures, and not thinking about anything else. *I no longer need to be on guard constantly. I don't have to continuously be part of his scheme of ways to get ahead at work. I no longer felt the push, the relentless pressure of what had to be done by such and such a time.*

Jimmy grunted and cursed out, "My God, I hated that about him!"

Jimmy continued with his review of his former soul: *Then there was the criticism. Oh yeah, the nonstop critique of others, thinking that he was superior to everyone, specifically his job at the trucking company. He thought his boss was a jerk and that his coworker, Darren, was incompetent. Oh and of course there was Gail in payroll who could never get his pay right. He thought his drivers were lazy and made his job more difficult than it needed to be. It wasn't just his coworkers that he criticized; there was the criticism of me!*

"Oh yeah," Jimmy muttered to himself, his expression contorting with discomfort as he dredged up the memories. "I hated it. That's when it became too much. Damn. I remember that day." His mind flashed back to the eventful day in July that served as the breaking point for him.

Chapter 4: The Unpleasant Memory of Jimmy's Former Soul

Friday, July 23, 1982 -- 12:50 pm

It was July 23rd. Jimmy remembered the date because it was the day before his thirty-first birthday. His soul was anxious as he had been waiting almost two weeks for his boss, Mr. Vanderheyden, to give him the news—the news of who would be promoted to senior dispatcher. On that day, something had happened to him while he sat alone at the table in the lunchroom. It was at that moment when he first felt the divide, an inner conflict that emerged. Even though his soul was sure he'd get the job, Jimmy's body was a bundle of nerves, muscles wound tight.

Stop it, Jimmy! Stop fidgeting. The Job's mine. That's what that voice kept saying, but it wasn't self-assurance; it was a struggle inside him. Despite the voice's insistence that he had the job, Jimmy's body wasn't convinced. It was like dance partners miss-stepping and blaming each other for it.

"Come on in, Jimmy," Mr. Vanderheyden grunted, gesturing his employee to take a seat in the uncomfortably low chair on the other side of his boss's desk. His boss was in his mid-forties, had a brush cut and a short mustache on a rather large, square head. The man wore suspenders and rolled-up sleeves. He was a stout man with an abrasive disposition. Mr. Vanderheyden was the stereotypical gruff boss; akin to a character played in a 1950s movie about a boss everyone despised.

"I've come to a decision," he said with a huff before crossing his arms and then resting them on his desk. "I've decided. I'm going with Darren," he finally said, meeting his employee's eyes. "I know you're a hard worker, but . . ." The middle-aged man hesitated, his gaze drifting away momentarily. He pushed his lower lip up with the muscles of his chin, nodding as if confirming a decision in his mind. "Well, I've made up my mind. I've given the job to Darren."

Jimmy's mouth hung open for a few seconds, a mix of disbelief and disappointment washing over him. Eventually, he closed it, a heavy silence lingering in the air. With a resigned nod, he rose from his seat. "OK," he finally managed to say.

Then, still in a state of shock, he slowly paced from his boss's office to his desk. It was only a minute after he sat when the voice started. *You can't be serious, Jimmy. You didn't get the job? Why did you just sit there with your mouth gaping wide open like a fish? Idiot! What the fuck did you do wrong?*

That's when Jimmy tensed up, the muscles in his neck and shoulders stiffened and his jaw clenched. The chatter in his head continued its nasty critique of his boss and co-workers. *Darren? Really? Of all people, incompetent*

Darren gets the job? Vanderheyden doesn't have a clue what he's doing. He sat motionless until the phone rang. He peered down at it momentarily before picking it up. "Jimmy, here."

"It's Sean." Sean's voice crackled through the receiver, urgency lacing his tone. "I'm at Motel 6. I've got my B.O.L's here but . . ."

Jimmy's voice cut in and concern edged his words, "But, what?"

"What's that FAX number again?" Sean's voice trembled slightly.

Jimmy's body was triggered by his soul's anger. He didn't like it, but he was being directed by his decision maker. He held the receiver tightly in his fist, gritting his teeth before he spoke: "For Christ's sake, man," he began but lowered his now shaky voice. "I've given you that number a million times."

He slammed the phone down and the sharp sound echoed, causing Darren to glance over and raise his eyebrows in surprise.

"I'll call him," Darren offered meekly.

"No. Don't. He needs to learn to write shit down or . . ."

Jimmy's frustration simmered, his voice trailing off as Darren thumbed towards Mr. Vanderheyden's office. "Shhh," Darren cautioned, nodding towards the closed door. "J.J.'s gonna hear ya."

"Who's J.J.?" Jimmy's curiosity piqued.

Darren brought his finger to his lips in a hushed gesture, then picked up the phone and dialed the driver's number.

After Darren's phone call, Jimmy sat quietly. Still feeling tense, he rubbed his face with his hands. From the corner of his eye, he noticed his co-worker staring at him.

"Stop looking at me," he said without turning. "I know you got the job, so, you can stop acting all nice."

5:45 pm

After work, Jimmy drove his green Saab 900 to the local grocery store. Once in, he maneuvered recklessly, bumping into patrons without saying "sorry" or "excuse me." He was on a mission to grab a roast chicken and leave. Anyone remotely in his way was going to get the wrath of a recently un-promoted young man. Although nobody obstructed his path, he did encounter a delay at the check-out as an elderly couple ahead of him appeared to be searching for change.

"Jesus Christ," he cursed under his breath.

With the steam of the chicken creating a hot, sweaty moisture on his right hand, his impatience grew as the old man continued to fumble through his wife's purse without result. Jimmy cocked his head to his right and tapped the floor with his foot. He peered up at the ceiling, listening to the woman speak to her husband.

"Walter!" the woman's voice rang out agitatedly. "Fifty-nine dollars and forty-nine cents. We have the money."

"I heard her, Bea. I forgot my glasses at home and the cabbie's waiting," the man replied, his tone tinged with frustration.

The old man's hands shook as his fingers fumbled through the bills, his movements slow and uncertain without the aid of his glasses.

"Come on, lady," Jimmy snapped, his patience wearing thin. "Take the Goddammed wallet from him."

The woman turned rather slowly, her plaster-white face contrasting sharply with her dark sunglasses. "Mind your manners, young man," she retorted curtly.

Before Jimmy could rudely respond, his attention was drawn to the cashier's voice coming from the empty lane next to him.

"I can take the next customer," she offered.

Jimmy marched over to the empty register, clutching his box of chicken tightly, "Finally."

Meanwhile, Jimmy's soul seethed with frustration upon discovering a brand-new dent on the passenger-side fender.

"Fuck!" he muttered under his breath in irritation.

6:15 pm

Once he was home, he placed his chicken on a ceramic dish and haphazardly shoved the dish into the oven, slamming the door. He plopped himself down onto the couch with such force that the springs beneath him clanked loudly, protesting the sudden weight.

"God damned couch," he muttered under his breath, his palm smoothing over his backside.

He leaned forward with his face in his hands, rubbing his face, soothing the tightness around his brow and then to his jawbone. He flexed his neck back making a feeble attempt to massage the tight muscles. That's when the telephone rang.

"Arg!" he grunted to himself before reluctantly picking up the phone. "Jimmy here," he answered abruptly, then squeezed his eyelids tight, realizing his blunder. "I mean... hello," he corrected himself.

"Haha. Hi, Jimmy. Remember me?" a female voice responded, amusement evident in her tone.

Jimmy clicked his tongue against his teeth, "Who is this?" he replied rudely.

"It's Susan," came the reply, her tone shifting to match his. "You don't recognize my voice?"

"Sorry," Jimmy said. "It's been a rough day."

"You mean... another rough day?" she replied. "You seem to have a lot of those lately."

"Yeah," Jimmy admitted as he sank back against the couch. "Anyway, what's up?"

"What's up? What kind of response is that? I'm going to come by and take you out for your birthday tomorrow. We made plans, remember?"

Jimmy tilted his head back in frustration, closing his eyes briefly. "Ah, shit. I forgot about that."

"Doesn't sound like you're all that keen on me coming over."

"Listen. I don't know if I'm in the mood for all that," Jimmy began with a groan while running his hand over his face. "I just got the news that I lost out on the promotion and now there's a fucking dent in my car that I just bought..."

He paused before his voice could get angrier. "Just... not this weekend, OK?"

There was a heavy silence on the other end of the line.

"Hello?" Jimmy prompted.

"OK, Jimmy," came the eventual response, followed by the abrupt click of the line disconnecting, leaving behind only the faint hum of a dial tone.

"Ah, shit," Jimmy muttered under his breath as he slammed the phone down onto the receiver.

8:30 pm

Jimmy was exhausted from the day's events. His muscles and joints were tight and sore from holding in his stress. He wanted nothing more than to shut out the noise in his head and just forget about what happened. He wanted to rest and simply lie in bed and forget the entire ordeal, but he couldn't. His soul wouldn't have any part of that. *You've got to get on Vanderheyden's good side, Jimmy. Maybe you need to be kissing ass more like Darren does. And that dent. Of all the places, you decided to park there?*

Jimmy's body knew it was time.

Chapter 5: gHost Road – Jimmy's Soul

Sunday, August 29, 1982 -- 5:00 pm

It was incredibly strange and unsettling, watching my body ride away from me.

I'm dead. Is this how it happens; one watching his body separate from himself? No. This can't be happening. But if I'm not dead, then... "what's going on?"

As the realization washed over me, I felt a profound sense of detachment, and I realized that I no longer had the physical capacity to express anxiety. The connection to him was broken. Typically, when I exhibited anxiety, my body would respond to it. When Jimmy left, my mind swirled with emotions, and I felt utterly powerless to express them. *I don't care for this at all! Am I just a mind now? Or perhaps a spirit? Is this what it's like to be a soul without a body?*

Despite my confusion, I knew my top priority was to find a way to reconnect with my body, to be reunited with Jimmy. I had to believe this was just a temporary setback. I had to believe I could fix it.

When I attempted to move as a bodiless soul, it was unnatural at first. I could no longer exert my legs and push my feet onto the earth. The only way I could was to concentrate. When my mind focused on moving forward,

I did. It was unusual, gliding through the air with no resistance. My initial movements weren't steady, but jerky, identical to the first time driving a manual transmission. Once I got into a rhythm, I moved freely. If I had to describe my speed, it was that of a casual jog, but no faster.

This is strange. I can't feel anything. The grass that would have normally brushed against my shins didn't create any sensation whatsoever. The physicality of touch or any other external sensation that I had experienced in a bodily state has disappeared.

When I arrived at the end of the dirt road, I discovered something interesting; someone had spray-painted a lowercase "g" in front of the "H" on the Host Road sign.

"Huh!"

I stopped and tried to sniff the air instinctively. But there was nothing. I couldn't smell anything and I couldn't register any scent. The absence of the familiar cow manure odor struck me. Though the stink was etched into my memory from before, I could no longer experience any aroma or fragrance. It was like a sensory void, leaving me feeling strangely disconnected from my surroundings.

I hovered where gHost Road and River Road met, contemplating my situation. I floated in mid-air, deliberating whether I was comfortable in a bodiless state. Perhaps I need to accept being an invisible entity.

My movement was slow but steady and seemingly effortless, which was disconcerting. What was even more unsettling was that my own "body" had vanished completely. I tried to wave my arms, but there was nothing there. I didn't even feel the sensation of limbs. It was like I was just a floating presence, moving forward freely. As I floated along, the occasional car passed by, not bothering to swerve around me.

An hour must have passed and I reached town. My invisibility was confirmed when I moved by the corner gas station where my neighbor Mrs. Austen rushed out with a paper bag in her grasp. Not even a flinch of acknowledgment. *This will definitely take some getting used to. I'm not exactly thrilled about it, but it doesn't seem like I have much of a choice.*

Wait a minute! Maybe if I yell something.

"Mrs. Austen!" I called out loudly, hoping for a response. But there was nothing, not even a glance in my direction.

Maybe I am dead. No, that can't be right. I can still think and speak, well... to myself at least.

I continued onto Bridge Street passing the streetlights that held the iconic neon fish signs mid-way up its posts. Surprisingly, I enjoyed the journey, even though the effort was underwhelming. By the time I arrived home, the sun had almost set. The coos of the pigeons that collected on the rooftop of my neighbor's house caused me to shift sideways to view them.

6:30 pm
From habit, my mind intended for me to reach for my key, but there was nothing to grab onto and even if there was, I wouldn't have been able to pick it up. Standing in front of my locked door, I realized there was only one thing to do – move through it!

Once inside, I toured the house as if it were my first time; the sensation was surreal. I lingered just inside the front door, taking in the layout of the house. Directly ahead was the hallway leading to the kitchen. To the left, I could see the dining room and living room, although the couch was partially hidden by the hallway wall. To my right, the staircase beckoned me to the second floor.

As I floated up the stairs, the steps remained eerily silent, devoid of the usual creaks and snaps. Panic began to creep in as I realized what I would have to face once I reached the top. Finally, I stood outside the bathroom door, hesitant to approach. Peering into the mirror, I caught a glimpse of the bathroom window reflected in the glass. Slowly, I edged closer to the vanity. As I moved in front, all I could see was the outline of a shower curtain.
There was no "me," no familiar image that I'd stared at so many mornings while I got ready for work. My face and my body had vanished from existence. It seemed odd because my first intuition was to cry and enter a melancholy state, but I couldn't. I didn't have the physical

means to express it. I still harbored the feelings, though. When I made my way down the stairs and to the living room, I found Jimmy sitting on the couch, engrossed in the news. His right arm was wrapped in a towel-covered ice pack, pressed against his head, while the other lay idly at his side. He turned ever so slowly, and for a moment... I wondered if he could see me.

"What are you doing here?" he asked, still seated. His narrowing with suspicion. His face twisted in annoyance. "Get out!"

"Why?" I hesitated.

"You're not part of me anymore..." His voice trailed off, his expression growing pensive as if grappling with his next words. "...and you're no longer welcome."

"What do you mean, not welcome?"

"Oh, sure," Jimmy replied matter-of-factly, his tone tinged with bitterness. "You really have no idea what imprint you've left on me, do you?"

"Imprint?" I echoed, puzzled by his cryptic words.

"Yes, you left an imprint... and not a nice one. A negative one." Jimmy's gaze turned distant, lost in memories. "As a matter of fact," he paused, his posture straightening with resolve. "...you don't recall this? 'There's no use for people like him in this town, is there, Jimmy?'" he said in a mocking voice, his words laced with resentment. "Or how 'bout this? 'You can't be serious, Jimmy. You didn't get the job? What the fuck did you do wrong?' That's why I never answered you. I never agreed with you." He sneered. "I was stuck with you and now I ain't!"

Ain't? I've never used that word. I hovered in the living room, silent, before saying: "But... I belong here. This is my house."

Jimmy appeared to be distracted by the television, blankly staring at it before turning back around. "Fine! Just stay away from me." Spit flung from his teeth.

I thought about his wish. It didn't really matter to me as my desire for warmth and comfort had disappeared. I glanced around the dimly lit kitchen, noticing the cobwebs in the corner. With a resigned sigh, I slithered away from him, settling in the shadows beside the neglected corners. *Jeez, Jimmy, you should have done a better job of cleaning.*

Monday, August 30, 1982 -- 6:30 am

I waited near the front door much like a dog waits for its owner to let him out, fluttering there until the early hours in the morning. Becoming impatient, I would shift back and forth in a pacing motion from the bottom of the stairs to the living room, where the clock was situated. Finally, 6:30 am came. I didn't hear him stirring, so I drifted upstairs. There was no movement from my former body, so I hovered over him and yelled, "Wake up!"

"Jesus Christ!" He jumped up, swinging his fists in midair. "You scared the hell out of me."

"You're going to be late."

Jimmy flung his sheets off of himself, his movements becoming more frantic.

"Get away from me. Wait downstairs or something," he muttered, his voice tense with irritation.

"Fine," I said with a huff.

I remained at the front door as I had earlier in the morning. Jimmy was taking longer than normal, so I checked the living room clock and ascended the stairs to find him still shaving.

"You're going to be late."

Jimmy snapped, "Piss off and wait downstairs."

Piss off? Another term I've never used.

7:30 am

Jimmy's disposition had not changed. He was curt and cold and unrelenting, but he allowed me to linger in the passenger seat as he drove to work. I studied his movements as he shifted the gearbox from first to second, jerking the car as he did.

"Come on, Jimmy. That wasn't very smooth!"

He half glanced in my direction but didn't respond. I wanted to explain how he should have released the clutch slower, but I could tell he wasn't in the mood for any more of my advice, so instead I tried a topic of neutral ground.

"So, tell me," I said, breaking the awkward morning silence. "How is it that you can see me?"

"I can't," he said, still looking ahead while sitting on the torn fabric seats of the Saab. "But I know you're there. I can sense you and unfortunately, I can still hear you."

I didn't respond immediately. Instead, I glanced out of the window, watching the familiar streets pass by in a blur. The morning light cast long shadows across the road.

As we continued the journey in silence, I couldn't help but feel a pang of sadness. The once-familiar routine of our daily commute now felt foreign and disjointed, a stark reminder of the rift between us. We'd spend about ten minutes on County Road 2 then onto number 38, which brought us to Highway 7; that's when Jimmy piped up.

"You hear that?" Jimmy's voice cut through the monotony of the road noise.

"Hear what?" I asked, trying to listen, but the hum of the engine drowned out any other sound.

My former body slowed the car, pulling off onto the gravel shoulder with a crunch, and then shut off the engine.

"What? What's going on?" I asked, my confusion mounting as Jimmy exited the car without a word. I joined Jimmy at the rear of the car.

"What's the problem?" I asked, scanning the vehicle for any visible signs of trouble.

Jimmy crouched down, his movements deliberate as he inspected the underside of the car. The passing cars kicked up dust, swirling around us as we examined the vehicle.

"I think it's an exhaust rattle," Jimmy muttered.

"I didn't hear anything."

Jimmy stood up, wiping his hands on his jeans before saying, "Stay here. I'm going to start the car. Let me know where it's coming from."

"OK," I replied, hovering nearby as Jimmy returned to the driver's seat and started the engine.

I hovered as low as I could, taking a good look at the tailpipe when my former physical body started the car followed by gravel flying in my direction. He was gone!

When the dust settled, I glanced back at the last image of my green Saab traveling west along Highway 7.

"What the hell? Is he losing his mind or something?"

With a resigned sigh, I floated in mid-air, unsure of what to do next. I pondered my options. "Well . . . he'll just have to manage things on his own," I glided toward Hastings, not through my usual paved route, but "as the crow flies," through farmers' fields and residents' backyards.

Once I arrived back on County Road 2, I stopped and recognized the grass escarpment where I ascended the previous week. *I wonder if I can find that house?* I slithered up to the top of the incline. The abandoned farmhouse stood right before me, immediately catching my eye. I continued to the front door, and then stopped. I could have easily drifted back into that house but didn't. *No. I better not.* I drifted away and moved toward the wooden fence where two Holsteins grazed. I'd only seen them up close once before when I rode by. I remembered how they just stared at me with their big brown eyes, watching as I passed. But when I approached them in my new state, they snorted and trotted away.

"Can they see me? No. No, they couldn't," I mumbled as I observed the creatures. They ambled off a few yards, stopping suddenly and turning to stare in my direction. With a hesitant step forward, I attempted to approach them once more, however; they seemed disturbed by my presence, emitting grunts and snorts that sounded eerily like horses. They eventually galloped off to join the others.

Fascinating. It's as if they have a sixth sense, unlike humans!

Deciding to leave the Holsteins be, I pressed on toward River Road. I was eager to conduct another experiment. Floating along the road, I soon reached the crest of a hill. There, my old nemesis, lay sprawled on the front lawn.

"Here, boy," I called out, cautiously approaching the canine that had always barked and chased after me along the fence.

The border collie jumped onto all fours, gave a sharp bark, and then backed away, growling as he did.

"What's wrong, boy," the owner called from the garage. The dog didn't stop glaring at me. *It sensed me all right.* It stepped farther away as I approached.

"Who's scared now, huh?" I taunted.

"What's gotten into you?" The owner emerged from his garage, squinting in my direction, unaware of my presence. "You see a ghost or something?"

"It's okay, boy. Just testing you," I reassured the dog before resuming my journey into town.

Once at the four corners, I decided to gallivant around the streets. I was quiet, but I soon got tired of the inactivity so decided to start yelling at the town's citizens.

"Hey!" I called to a middle-aged woman, crossing the street in a hurry after exiting the gas station.

Nothing.

Then, with courage, I called out to a burly man. His shoulders were broad and clad in a biker vest, he seemed headed towards Brewers Retail. "Hey, dummy!" I called out, but there was still no response.

I continued these silly antics for another fifteen minutes. It was humorous, but the novelty soon wore off. In fact, while I hovered around town with no one to communicate with, I will admit, I began to feel lonely. This was unusual because there were moments in my human world when I would have enjoyed the solitude. Yes, I would have enjoyed being left alone, not being bothered by anybody or anything, but at that moment, floating in the middle of the four corners, I didn't care for it at all. I certainly couldn't embrace it as I thought I could. It wasn't anything I hoped it would be. The only human who could sense me was my former human self, but he was at work and wanted nothing to do with me.

I continued drifting around town, listening in on random pedestrian conversations, but that got boring too, so I just went home.

As I arrived at the front of the house, I checked the position of the sun, estimating it to be around one or two in the afternoon. Standing in front of my door, I paused briefly before a realization struck me.

"What was I thinking?" I muttered to myself. "Just go through the wall!" With that, I mustered my resolve and prepared to pass through the barrier without hesitation.

Once through I discovered that Jimmy was home, sitting on the couch.

"Why are you home so early?" I asked, puzzled by Jimmy's unexpected return.

Jimmy sat there, seemingly lost in a daze, his gaze fixed ahead as if he hadn't fully awakened yet.

"Why did you take off without me?" I pressed.

He finally turned to face me. His blank stare was concerning, so much so that I shifted to look behind me. He eventually replied, "They sent me home." His motor skills appeared to be delayed. His words came off his tongue slowly.

"What? Why?"

There was a prolonged silence before Jimmy finally spoke, his words slow and hesitant. "They said I was acting strange. They were worried, so... they sent me home... in a cab. I..." He trailed off, struggling to articulate his thoughts.

"What?"

"I... couldn't remember what to do," Jimmy confessed, his voice devoid of its usual vigor. "I found myself staring at the phone... not knowing what to do."

"You know damn well what to do," I interjected.

"It's... it's not that," Jimmy insisted, turning to stare blankly at the dark TV screen, his hands resting limply in his lap. After a brief pause, he added, "I think I'm feeling it."

"Feeling what?" I asked impatiently.

With another delay, he eventually turned and answered, "Not having a soul. There's nothing. I feel like . . . there's nothing to live for." He turned to stare at the blank TV again. "There's no purpose. I knew you were driving me, but . . ." he thought for a moment, then turned back to face me. "I don't want you." He continued. "I need to find a good soul."

"What do you mean? What the hell's wrong with me?" I demanded.

Jimmy shook his head, his expression troubled. " No. No. I don't want yours back. I left you by the side of the road for a reason. I can't take it anymore. I can't take *you* anymore. I need to find a good soul," he explained, his words coming out quicker and more articulate.

I hovered in the living room, absorbing his irrational remarks. It seemed that the longer he was away from me, the more he became a soulless body, devoid of thought or conscience. *He needs me. But could he really find another soul? Was that even possible?*

"You'd better come to work with me tomorrow," Jimmy suddenly blurted out.

I was taken aback by the invitation. *Maybe he's regaining himself. Maybe he's feeding off me.*

"Yes, I think I should."

"I don't want to get fired."

"Uh... all right."

"But if you're going to stay here, go in the basement. You're too close for me to feel comfortable," Jimmy instructed.

"If you wish," I acquiesced.

* * *

I listened carefully as his footsteps creaked up the wooden stairs and to his bedroom. I hovered just inside the basement door directly below the staircase. After twenty minutes or so the tossing and turning of my former body stopped; this was evident from the lack of squeaks from the cheap bed frame that I purchased when I moved in.

Tuesday, August 31, 1982 -- 7:10 am

Jimmy was kind enough to open the door to ensure I made it into the rear of the cab with him. I didn't have the heart to tell him he didn't need to. Throughout the morning, he had been surprisingly pleasant, but I couldn't shake the feeling that he was up to something. Deep down, he knew he needed me, or else his days on earth were numbered. He wasn't the only one whose existence was in jeopardy; so was mine. *If he could find another soul, who knows what would happen to me?*

* * *

Jimmy paid the cabbie and I slithered behind him and up the stairs into that dingy hallway that led us to the dispatch office. It was a well-lit office but in disrepair. There was a long window stretching the length of the office, which presented a full view of the derelict factory next door; the remnants of dingy restaurant equipment stored outside along the adjoining fence. The window also gave Mr. Vanderheyden a good view of what tractors and trailers were still parked in the yard. Many times, he would stroll out into the dispatch office, stand behind me, find the trailer number, grumble something under his breath, then march back into his office and slam the door. The office housed the three of us: me, Darren and Leslie, who worked in accounting.

"Hey, Jimmy," Darren said as he strolled in. "Feeling better?"

Even though our connection was severed, I found myself speaking on behalf of my body. It was an unusual sensation, likely due to our proximity. I sensed that he needed me to step in, so I took over.

"Yeah, thanks. Anything I need to know?" I replied, adopting a matter-of-fact tone.

"Gallagher is headed to Sarnia. His load still needs to be cleared. I called the broker first thing, not knowing if you were..."

"I'm here, aren't I?"

Darren picked up his pen and continued entering data into his daily log. I always thought him to be nosey and his comments unnecessary.

With Jimmy settled in his seat, I floated around like a balloon, bobbing in midair. I shifted from side to side, inspecting Jimmy's scribbles and nudging him toward the next task. It wasn't effortless, but it was manageable. It felt akin to maneuvering a robot with a remote control. It would have been far easier if we were together once again, but we weren't. I made the best of it to get us through the day.

* * *

We continued to function as a team, physically and analytically; in this way, Jimmy and I performed our daily duties without issue. Mr. Vanderheyden checked in occasionally at which point I lied for him. Jimmy mentioned he had an inner ear infection that made him feel "off" the previous day. This stopped the incessant prodding that was beginning to annoy me. But something interesting happened that morning; something that I didn't expect. I'm not even sure if Jimmy expected it to take place. When requiring the use of the men's room at lunchtime, Jimmy left while I remained at the desk; that's when Darren whispered to Leslie.

"Jesus Christ. I prefer the 'vegetative-state' Jimmy was in yesterday to this snarky asshole that showed up today."

"I know," she replied, her voice barely above a whisper. "I don't know how the hell you put up with him for so long."

Darren shook his head before picking up his ringing phone.

I was angry at Darren for his comment. Initially, I wanted to lash out at him as soon as Jimmy returned, but something changed as soon as my former body arrived at his desk. I sort of . . . felt sorry for him. I could compare it to being the father of a young boy, having witnessed the boy's friends talking behind his son's back while not knowing I was the father. *Is this really what people think of him?*

I stewed in frustration for the remainder of the day and made no attempt to talk to Jimmy about it, let alone even bring it up.

* * *

Once we got home, I slithered to the basement, which had become my usual place of late. I didn't mind it there. I can't say that was the case when I first moved in as it was a typical creepy century home basement. I remember when I first moved into the house; I ventured to the basement to replace a fuse. I was immediately taken aback by the low ceiling, lit only by two incandescent bulbs, their fixtures unstable as they were never affixed to the floor joists. The shadow from the piles of boxes left distorted images against the wall of the large irregularly shaped rocks of the fieldstone foundation. The dampness also attracted a multitude of spiders, dead and alive. The long thin legs of a Daddy long-leg spiders occupied most corners.

That day, the lights weren't on, but there was a thin stream of daylight from the basement window that barely illuminated the surroundings. Although no longer bothered by the eeriness of it while in my soul-state, I certainly didn't care for visiting it while in Jimmy's body.

* * *

The gossip didn't stop on Tuesday; it continued all week long whenever Jimmy stepped away from his desk. Even if there weren't any negative comments while Jimmy was absent, there was certainly much eye-rolling and sneering from his co-workers, implying their discontent. There wasn't much communication between Jimmy and me during that period. I still struggled to understand why he was disliked and more so, why he never got promoted in the first place. I was certain my former carriage had given the wrong vibe with his body language, or perhaps wasn't looking his boss in the eyes enough to gain his trust. Maybe he wasn't gesturing properly when expressing himself, or maybe he was just failing to explain facts clearly.

I racked my brain all week trying to pin that lack of respect from others onto him, concocting the narrative that this was purely Jimmy and his lack of couth and awareness to be able to be accepted in a social setting. I was stubborn, and despite everything I saw at the trucking firm, I struggled to admit it: they didn't dislike Jimmy—it was me they had a problem with!

It was at that moment that it sank in. If I wasn't with him, such as the time he took off on me, he entered into a vegetative state. When I was with him, his co-workers disliked him. Not only that, Jimmy hated me and wished me to disappear.

Although it was difficult to fully admit, I eventually came to the conclusion that Jimmy had every right to ditch me.

Saturday, September 4, 1982 -- 12:32 am

It had been almost a week since I became disembodied. I had hovered in my usual spot, underneath the stairs in the basement, resting my mind when I determined that Jimmy was fast asleep and not in need of me, so I took a risk. I ventured out into the night, away from my former body. I needed something, something more than being rejected all week, so there I was, out on Bridge Street – in the bleak night. It was peaceful. The moon was still climbing in the clear dark sky, the odd star twinkled at me when I scanned upward. The night was still, not that I could feel any breeze, but I determined it to be so by the lack of movement in the branches and leaves. The pigeons across the street resonated with a soft gurgling coo, which was soothing. It was comforting knowing I hadn't disrupted them. I suppose they'd gotten used to me already.

I continued gliding down Bridge Street and over the river to the four corners, stopping in front of the bank. It was then that it occurred to me that Jimmy hadn't ventured out on his bike since that fateful day. *Is that because he didn't want me tagging along, or maybe . . . he was worried that we'd somehow become reconnected again. I wonder.*

While hovering at the four corners, still contemplating my thoughts regarding Jimmy, I heard a faint call that stirred me.

"What's that?"

I followed the sound of the woman's voice, leading me towards the far end of Front Street, an area I rarely visited in my embodied state. As I floated along, the voice grew clearer, guiding me closer to the imposing presence of the water tower that overlooked the tannery. With each step, the urgency in the woman's tone became more apparent. I arrived at the intersection of Wellington and Front, where the voice seemed to emanate from. *Who could be calling out to me in this part of town?*

This woman's ability to evoke me was enticing, something I hadn't experienced in that state. *I'm wanted. Someone is calling me. My spirit is being called upon. There! That's the house.*

In front of me stood a small brick bungalow, which I guessed had been built in the 1920s. The main floor was dark, however there was a low light coming from the basement window. *That's where the call is coming from.* I sifted through the front door and easily maneuvered through the small house and down to the darkened basement where I discovered four elderly people sitting on each side of a card table; there were three women and a man. Their faces were lit by the orange glow of two strategically placed candles. The three women appeared to be in their seventies, the man in his early eighties. The woman facing me had brightly dyed red hair and wore a pair of large sunglasses, covering her rather small, pale, emotionless face. The woman to her left had white hair, which appeared freshly permed, containing a tinge of blue. The woman to her right was incredibly tiny. Her body was perfectly proportioned to that of a ten-year-old girl; her feet didn't touch the ground. Her eyes were open while the others remained closed. The other three had their hands placed on a small heart-shaped piece of wood, on which the tips of their fingers carefully rested. The heart-shaped piece was on a wooden plank, displaying the alphabet, numbers one to nine, a zero, a simple "Yes," a "No" and finally "Goodbye."

When I shifted closer, I got a better visual of the man; he was tall and frail. He wore bifocals and had little hair, combed perfectly over the bald part of his head. His skin hung, forming saggy jowls. *I've seen him somewhere before – the woman with the red hair too.*

"It's here," the woman with sunglasses called out. "Walter. I can feel it."
"Go on, Beatrice," the man across from her said. He inhaled slowly before continuing, "Call out to it."

"Ask it something, Bea," the blue-haired nodded eagerly.

All but the small woman's eyes remained closed.

"Hello? Beatrice." I called. "Can you hear me?"

"Yes," the red-haired woman replied.

The woman to Beatrice's left glanced at her with furrowed brows, "Who are you talking to?" she whispered, leaning in closer to hear Beatrice's response.

Beatrice focused on the presence she sensed, ignoring the whispered question.

"Yes, I can hear you," Beatrice replied.

"Bea?" the man interjected.

Ignoring the interruption, Beatrice held up a hand, silencing the others. "Shhhh, everyone," she insisted.

She removed her hand from the wood piece and pointed her trembling finger toward me. "He's right there!"

The other two opened their eyes, following where the woman was pointing. I knew they couldn't see me, given their immediate returned glares back at the woman wearing sunglasses.

"What is it?" Walter asked, continually staring at her.

The woman stood and grabbed her white cane. Walter

also came to his feet.

"Don't," Beatrice said and waved him away with her free hand.

I remained still in the air as the woman's attention shifted toward me.

Taking cautious steps closer, the woman with the sunglasses fixed her gaze on me. "You are a lost soul," she declared.

With a deliberate motion, the woman extended her hand toward me, her palm almost grazing the empty space where I hovered. "You're different from the others," she remarked. "You're not dead, are you?"

"No," I managed to reply, grateful for the opportunity to communicate with her.

Her expression softened slightly as she nodded in understanding. "No, I didn't think so." Leaning on her cane for support, the woman rested her hands atop its curved handle. "It's dangerous for you to be without your other self," she cautioned, her tone grave. "Don't remain dissociated from your body for too long; otherwise. . . ," She raised her finger. ". . . you'll be a lost soul forever. The demon spirits will easily find you."

Walter shifted uneasily in his chair, his eyes darting nervously between Beatrice and the unseen presence she claimed to communicate with. "Beatrice, you're scaring me," he pleaded.

With a dismissive wave of her hand, Beatrice brushed off Walter's concerns. "Oh, shush," she chided him. "I'm speaking with a spirit."

Turning her gaze back toward me, Beatrice posed a question. "What is your name?"

I responded tentatively, "Jimmy. You . . . you sense me?"

"I can, but you mustn't stay long."

Feeling a glimmer of hope at her words, I hesitated before asking, "Can I... can I come to visit you another time?"

"Yes, yes," Beatrice agreed readily. "But... you are in danger. You need to reunite with your body... before it's too late."

Her warning hung in the air as a reminder of the precarious situation I found myself in.

Monday, September 6, 1982 – 3:30 am

Although I took the blind woman's advice seriously, I still felt the need to get out of that dank basement that was once my house, so out again I went.

There was something about the middle of the night that inspired me. It was the only time I felt alive. I wasn't scared. Maybe I should have been but I wasn't. I slithered down the road; the raccoons scattered when they sensed me, which I found humorous. As I made my way through the neighboring backyards, the sound of a dog barking pierced the quiet of the neighborhood which would trigger a chorus of other barks in response. In my human days, such disturbances used to irritate me; but now, as a wandering spirit, I oddly found myself enjoying the chaotic symphony of barks echoing through the night.

I coasted through the four corners and then to Wellington and Front Street, but Beatrice wasn't signaling for me. Although a little disappointed, it didn't stop me from finding entertainment elsewhere. I continued west until Front Street turned into River Road. That's when I decided to slink through the trailer part, with the hopes of another human calling a spirit. I moved between the multitude of trailers: nothing but a single human warming his hands close to the embers of a fire pit. I believed it to be Fred, but I wasn't sure, as he fled quickly when I caught the attention of a German Shepard; its piercing bark startled him. The dog's owners stirred while in the comfort of their trailer, so I left the park and carried on up the road, prowling along it as if I hadn't a care in the world, knowing full well that my continued travel would take me to that infamous road.

I hovered at the trailer park exit momentarily, as I would

in a vehicle, scanning left and right — but I didn't move. Something caught my attention along River Road. I saw what appeared to be a man bent over, carrying a large object on his back walking along the road. The lights from the trailer park scarcely illuminated the figure, creating a faint silhouette of a hunched-over man with a large sack weighing him down, his shoes dragging along the pavement. His movement seemed strained but his pace was steady. I hesitated for a moment, unsure of what to do. The figure seemed so focused, almost oblivious to my presence. "Hey!" I called out. With a growing sense of frustration, I raised my voice again, hoping to break through. "Hey, you!" I repeated. The image didn't waver from its duty.

Once in the clearing and out from the tall trees that sheltered him from the moonlight, his appearance became clearer. He was a middle-aged man, grimacing as he passed. His tense face and the grit he expressed were that of an individual possessed by his task. Whatever assignment he took on that night, however unpleasant it may have been; it was clear to him what his purpose was.

"Hey! Can you hear me?" I called in vain.

Without waiting for a response, I decided to follow. *This is just...* I thought to myself... *this is just like the dream I had last month.* I recalled the motion, the effort — that unquestionable struggle required to carry that load, but to where? I woke before I finished my duty in my dream. The memory returned; that unfulfilled sensation I had. I remembered the emptiness of not accomplishing my obligation as if I had let him down. But . . . who was "him", and what the hell was in that bag?

The man maintained his steady pace, so I glided along, matching his speed until he continued onto that road – gHost Road. I stopped at the end of it, watching his heavy, clunky walk, uninterrupted by the unevenness of the dirt road he traveled through. The moon had provided a clear path for him. Before I could even decide to follow, he passed another man returning from the house; neither of the two acknowledged each other. *Strange.* The man heading toward me held an empty bag. His appearance was different from the first. He was rugged and broader. He seemed to stare right through me. The whites of his eyes surrounded his dark menacing pupils. His expression held an undeniable disgust, a repulsion; not from where he came, no, it was deeper, something from within, much like someone who had just committed a heinous crime but felt it was somehow justified. Although he couldn't see me, I still found it difficult to face him.

Then came another; this figure came from the same direction as the first, from River Road, also carrying a sack, but this person was much smaller in stature. *Is it . . . is that a woman?*

I hovered still at the corner of River and gHost Road, watching that woman dragging the soles of her boots on the pavement; the scratchy, scraping sound was unsettling. Her steps were mechanical and methodical.

Once closer, she also maintained a stern determined expression, as if the mission was to be completed without hesitation and with precision. She was driven. Driven by what, I wasn't sure, but she wouldn't stop. There was no way of interfering with any of them. I felt like I was trapped in one of those bad dreams you can't wake up from, where every step feels heavy and every move is sluggish. The sound of scraping and dragging filled the air.

"Who are you?" I asked, gliding along beside her.

Part of me wanted to get away from the scene. For a moment, I managed to tear myself away from it, but curiosity quickly pulled me back in. I had to know what they were doing.

I glided along the grass, keeping up with the woman's pace. Her warm breath entered the cool night air as she trudged along the path to the old farmhouse which, upon my scanning ahead, was occupied. There was a low glow coming from the basement window. Beside the window was a long metal chute angled downward into the basement. The opening was held open by a wooden stick. Once in front of the house, I heard a grunt as the first man flung his sack onto the ground in front of a metal chute. The woman waited for the man whose movements seemed almost automated. He shifted the sack onto the edge of the chute, pulling it up to release what appeared to be coal, gravity carrying the lumps of coal into the basement. He then turned and marched back to River Road, staring straight ahead, not making eye contact with the woman. In turn, the woman mirrored the same motion, exhaling heavily as she carefully lowered the bag to the ground. Its dusty coal cascaded onto the chute with a muted clatter. With practiced efficiency, she adjusted her stance and retraced her steps back to River Road, the empty sack dangling from her hand like a forgotten accessory.

I moved closer to the farmhouse, hovering low so that I could investigate what was happening on the other side of the basement window. I couldn't see anything but the bright orange light coming from the open door of a coal furnace; its glowing embers lit up the room. But I did hear the sound of metal scraping on concrete. That scraping and shoveling continued a few more times before stopping. As I watched, someone closed the furnace door with a shovel, but then I couldn't see who it was – my view was obstructed. That was when I heard a hiss from outside the house.

"Huh?"

I even floated through to the Holsteins' fields, worried that the noise might have been because of me. I hovered there for a minute, listening carefully.

There it is again. What is that noise?
The haunting "hiss" sound was something I didn't care to hear again, so I coasted onto River Road, and into town, seeking refuge from the unsettling noise. The sound had

finally disappeared and also, to my relief, the ghoulish figures carrying their heavy loads of coal.

Wednesday, September 8, 1982 -- 3:07 am

Night after night I perused my small town seeking, searching for something—anything meaningful and uplifting. I had hoped Beatrice would call me but she didn't. I suppose there was no séance that night. There was nothing but a deserted Bridge Street; no cars, no pedestrians, just me. I crossed the dam and swerved onto Front Street to the park with the intent of getting a clear view of the reflection of the moon on the smooth river surface. I found it calming. I didn't miss human sightings at nighttime as they never interacted with me anyway.

I stayed at that location, beside the gazebo peering out at the still water, listening to the haunting wail of a distant loon's call. It was peaceful. Part of me asked if I even wanted to return to my house. It was then that I thought about everything that happened, especially at work. It was then that I thought about everything that happened, especially at work while Jimmy and I were temporarily parted and I was alone in the room with his co-workers. It was clear, they didn't appreciate him. *Never mind him; they weren't appreciative of me! I'm the one who molded him into what he is.*

It was at that moment, hovering alongside the quiet river that I accepted it. I accepted the fact that my bad behavior resulted in a lack of friends, a lover, and even camaraderie with co-workers. It was time to make a move. I needed to deal with this. *Yes. That's what I'll do. I'll have a conversation with Jimmy on the way to work and make every attempt to clean up my act and treat people with more respect.*

I decided to head home, so I moved along Front Street to the four corners. I didn't need to, but it was somewhat comforting to advance along the sidewalk. It brought back memories of my physical existence, but my nostalgic reverie was abruptly interrupted by the sight of a young man sprinting up Bridge Street. "Hey!" I called out instinctively. To my surprise, he swiveled in my direction, albeit briefly, before darting across the bridge. Determined, I gave chase, my curiosity piqued by the oddity of his translucent form, reminiscent of my own before I vanished from sight. *Can he sense me?*

"Stop! Wait." I called out but lost sight of him after he continued over the crest of the hill beyond where St. George's church stood.

When I arrived at the top, the image vanished completely. I circled the surroundings of my last sighting, determined to find him but was distracted by the blue and red lights of an ambulance; its piercing siren wailed as it sped past, eventually slowing to turn on Front Street. I hurried toward the four corners where I discovered that the emergency vehicle had stopped in front of the apartment building above the Fish and Chips restaurant. I followed the driver and paramedics up the stairs where a middle-aged woman, still in her nightgown, was shivering on the landing, stuttering and crying uncontrollably.

The woman's voice quivered as she pointed towards the upper level. "He's in the bathroom... in the bathroom." One of the paramedics nodded and gestured to his colleague. "Get that woman a blanket." As they ascended the stairs, the floorboards groaned beneath their weight, adding to the tension in the air.

My curiosity stopped there as I knew something horrible was going on. Even though I was invisible, I still felt I was intruding, so I retreated onto the street and joined the small crowd that formed, their faces lit up by the flashing lights. I stayed for a few minutes until a police vehicle arrived, pushing the crowd away from the entrance. I wanted to find out what happened but was worried about Jimmy hearing the noise and waking up without me, so I gravitated along Bridge Street and re-entered my house. After determining he was still asleep, I waited under the basement stairs until daybreak.

6:30 am

I shifted myself up to the main floor upon hearing the creaks of the floorboards from the bedroom. Jimmy made his usual trip to the washroom to relieve himself and then stomped down the stairs.

"Good morning," I said as I followed him to the kitchen where he prepared his coffee. He then stretched and leaned against the kitchen sink. I was about to tell him that there was some type of drama last night, but I thought – based on his lack of response to my "good morning" – that I'd better leave it be and let him wake; besides, I was going to wait until in the car to let him know that I admitted my faults and would try and become a better soul. That was the plan, but something was different. He was humming a song. He never hums in the morning. In fact, *I* never sang until at least ten o'clock when the coffee finally kicked in. Something was very different that day, so I decided to prompt him with my plan.

"You know," I started. He didn't respond. "Are you ignoring me?" I asked firmly, but there was still no reply. My former body swung around and filled his cup, added his cream and sugar, and proceeded upstairs to the shower.

"Jimmy," I called again from the other side of the bathroom door, this time with worrying tension. "I'm . . . I'm sorry for the way I've behaved."

He started singing "I Can't Go for That," so I lowered myself down the stairs and waited.

* * *

Once outside, Jimmy didn't leave the car door open as he normally would, which frustrated me, so I took a chance and didn't enter the vehicle, and yelled, "You're being an ass. Good luck. Don't get fired!"

He put the car into first and bolted out the driveway and down Bridge Street.

"To hell with him," I said and sifted my way toward town and eventually to the four corners. There was still a police vehicle situated in front of the apartment above the Fish and Chip restaurant. There was no officer inside it so I meandered around the town center in hopes of hearing something, but citizens bustled to and fro as if nothing happened, so I concluded that nothing of importance did and went on with my pursuit.

* * *

It had been just over a week in my bodiless state. I had become used to my new form, but I can't say I exactly enjoyed it. I missed the sense of touch. I missed romance, and as for heartache; strangely enough, I missed that too—it reminded me that I was alive. But, I suppose, those two came hand-in-hand. I certainly missed feeling loved and the warm sensation of receiving affection. *That's only a memory now,* I thought. I began to worry that I would forget what it was like.

The one thing I did notice, however, was the lack of Jimmy's pull when I gallivanted around town. It was weird, but I still felt the need to drift back to my brick house as I expected him to be sent home early again that day.

3:00 pm

Before going in, I checked the driveway to see if my green Saab was there. It wasn't, which meant Jimmy either hadn't come home yet or had been sent back in a cab by his boss once again. I floated through the front door. No sign of Jimmy. If he had been around, he'd usually be lounging on the couch by then.

I scampered towards the large living room window, the afternoon sun still fairly high in the sky, so I'd estimated it to be around 3:00 pm. The clock in the living room confirmed it.

"I wonder how he's making out."

I decided to float around the kitchen and watch the flies buzz against the hot windows that were illuminated by the intense sun. I had no idea how many insects occupied my house. There were tiny spiders that hung on their webs between the corner baseboards, ladybugs that walked upside down, glued to the kitchen ceiling and of course, the house flies begging to get out.

Maybe I should get out! Why am I even here? Is it morbid curiosity that brought me back? Was I hoping to return home and find my soulless body in a comatose state? And then what? Laugh at him? Poke fun at him? What exactly was I hoping to achieve?

* * *

After a few hours and gliding from room to room, I returned to the east window and waited. There was no sun as it had since moved west. That's when I noticed my green Saab roll in the driveway. *Finally,* I thought.

"Well?" I let out as he strolled through the front door, his demeanor unchanged. Still, he didn't acknowledge my presence. "What the hell's going on?" I demanded as I followed him into the kitchen, growing increasingly concerned.

Oh no. He really can't hear me. What happened?

It was at that moment that the memory flooded back to me—*the image I saw last night, that translucent figure of a young man scurrying up the street toward my house. Can it be? Can it be him that entered my former body? Did he die and take it over?*

I rushed out of the house and glided steadily down the street to the four corners, my mind racing with questions. *How do I find out what really happened to him?*

I hovered outside the Fish and Chip restaurant, peering up at the apartment above. I decided to enter it, gliding up to the second floor, and into the apartment where the same middle-aged woman was sitting in a rocking chair, staring out at the afternoon sun. I scanned the entire apartment to determine she was alone. I spun around in front of her. She had dark circles under her bloodshot eyes; they peered hopelessly outward as if searching for something.

"Lady, can you hear me?" I asked, hoping for some acknowledgment.

No answer.

I had nothing to lose, so I hovered in the woman's apartment, waiting for a sign, for something to spell out the truth. And finally, the phone rang.

"Hello," the woman answered in a tone weighed down by despair.

I could hear the faint voice of a man on the other end, but could only make out what the woman was saying.

"Oh, Charlie." The woman reached for a tissue, her hand trembling slightly. "Billy was so young." Her voice wavered as tears welled up in her eyes. "I know, I know. He struggled with narcotics. He promised he'd get off it."

There was a pause, filled only with the sound of the woman's stifled sobs.

"No. Not an overdose," she continued, her voice heavy with sorrow. "He drowned . . . in the tub. He took . . . well, whatever he took, he fell asleep in the tub."
The woman's body shuddered as it did the night before. "That's when I found him."

I strained to hear the faint, unintelligible voice respond from the other end of the line.

"Will you?" A pause. "Yes, Charlie. I could use the company," she said. "You've always been such a good friend. OK. Yes. I will try. OK. OK. I will see you Friday."

* * *

I made the motion to return home and to confirm Jimmy's transformation with Billy Gibson's soul. I had concluded that was his name as I checked the mailbox to the apartment -- it read Gibson. I also came to the conclusion that his spirit had entered my former body while I watched the drama that followed his death. I couldn't determine if he forced himself in while Jimmy was asleep or if he was welcomed in.

Entering through the front door, I found my former body standing in the kitchen, his movements methodical as he spread peanut butter on a slice of bread. Already dressed in cycling gear, he seemed absorbed in his pre-cycling routine, unaware of the profound shift that had occurred. I watched his mannerisms as he readied himself. He appeared less jittery and more tranquil, a calmness I didn't recognize. His breathing was evenly paced, not held in for moments followed by large exhales, as he did—as *I* did—for so long. For once, he appeared relaxed. I have to admit, I was jealous.

* * *

He flew down Bridge Street on his mountain bike so fast that I couldn't keep up, but I continued along his normal route, even though I lost sight of him momentarily. Once I passed St. George's church and then the bridge, I noticed he had stopped at the four corners. *He, I mean we've, never stopped there.* Upon my arrival, he was speaking with Big Al the bartender, so I hovered nearby. The afternoon sun cast a warm glow over the street.

"It's a dammed shame," Al said. "Drugs. I don't get it." His words lingered in the air, heavy with the weight of the recent tragedy.

Jimmy's brow furrowed as he absorbed the somber conversation. "Was he a good guy?"

Big Al nodded solemnly. "Yeah, very likable. Lived right above the Fish and Chips place." He gestured toward the historic brick building across the street, its facade weathered by time.

Jimmy followed Al's gaze, his expression thoughtful. When Al dropped his hand, Jimmy could sense the scrutiny in his friend's gaze.

"You seem different," Al observed, "Like... jollier or somethin'."
"Huh? What do you mean?"

Al shrugged, a faint smile tugging at his lips. "I don't know. Anyways, I've got to get to work. Stop in for a beer sometime."

"I will. Probably Friday," Jimmy replied, his thoughts lingering on Al's observation as he watched the barman waddle toward the pub entrance.

My former physical self headed west on Front Street. I continued at whatever speed I was able to make, cutting through backyards and ditches to catch up. When I did, I found him laboring up the hill and onto River Road. I watched him grit his teeth as he powered on up, beads of sweat produced on his forehead. I was envious of his effort and determination.

I suppose I did miss the temporary pain and gratification once I reached that goal, which must be exactly what he felt when he approached the hill's summit. The anticipation, the struggle, the surge of relief and pride—a mix of emotions that only those who have experienced it can truly understand. Gravity accelerated him ahead of my ability to keep up, so I watched as he sped down the hill and out of sight once again, worried that he might turn onto that godforsaken road. I panicked. I couldn't go any faster and there were no other options; I simply had to catch up. I eventually did; passing the mound of horse dung that had dried in the sun. He was stopped on River Road, under the gHost Road sign, scanning the farmhouse in the distance. He hadn't moved, which gave me enough time to catch up.

As I hovered around his motionless form, I pleaded desperately, "Don't do it. Go home." I attempted to push him away with whatever force I could muster. His eyes blinked rapidly for a second before reaching to rub his right arm to soothe where I had exerted my energy. He paused for what felt like an eternity, adjusting his bike and considering his options. Then, to my relief, he pivoted his bike around and pedaled away.

"Did he feel that?" I wondered aloud, even though I knew no one could hear me.

Despite lacking physical form, I still experienced a profound sense of relief. If I could have sighed, I would have, but even that was beyond my reach.

I watched my former self ride away. It was a poignant moment, realizing that I no longer needed to protect him. It felt akin to what a father might feel when letting his son drive off alone for the first time.

Before I made my move to turn, I took another glance at that house on gHost Road. I have to admit, it was disturbingly alluring.

* * *

Once in town, I decided not to return home. Instead, I hovered along the shore watching the last of the boats dock at the marina, their ripples cascading from where they docked to the riverbank in front of me. After the last crest leveled out, the water mirrored the sun's orange and pink late afternoon glow. As I contemplated, a memory stirred: the encounter on gHost Road with Jimmy. Could it be related? With no limbs to test my theory, I hovered as low as I could manage and gently exerted my energy on the water's surface. "I think it worked!" I exclaimed as it rippled ever so slightly. Yet, despite several attempts, I couldn't replicate the action.

9:00 pm

I spent hours practicing, trying to recreate the tiny ripple with the intention of somehow establishing a way to communicate with the living, even though I hadn't surrendered to the idea that I was dead. No. That conclusion wasn't acceptable to me. I still had feelings. I still had emotions. I retained memories as I did when I was in Jimmy's body. I could still transport myself. The only thing I lacked was the physical ability to communicate with humans. *That certainly doesn't define me as deceased, or does it?*

When the breeze picked up, I had to abandon practicing water movement, not just because I was no longer able to witness the movement, but because I became preoccupied with an odd movement a few yards away. As I watched, the figure materialized once more, this time about fifty yards further down the road. It was unlike anything I'd ever seen before, neither human nor animal. Its form seemed to shift and flow, almost ethereal in nature. Its smoky appearance shifted and changed in shape as it moved, simulating that of a squid navigating through the ocean.

I ventured out to engage with it but stopped when I lost sight of it. I remained motionless for a moment, hearing only the rushing noise coming from the dam, so I moved toward where I saw the metamorphosed object. It last appeared at the bend where Front Street turned into River Road. *I hear it again.* The same unsettling hiss filled the air once more, it stirred up a pool of memories within me. It was the same disturbing sound I heard at the farmhouse. That's when I became worried, so I backtracked through yards and the fence—the hissing sound followed me. It was close, so I darted through a clump of cedar bushes and back into town; the noise became louder, and its hiss transformed into an almost sinister growl, much like that of an angry dog chasing me. I felt certain it would pursue me further, but whatever it was, was interrupted by another noise – this time a welcoming one.

"Hey, Pal. You OK?"

"What?" I said, still experiencing the trepidation of the eerie noise that had suddenly disappeared. "You . . . you can see me?"

"I see lots of things," said Fred, the scraggly-looking man who had begged me for a cigarette a couple of weeks prior. His eyes bobbed with my movement.

"Something was chasing me."

"That was a demon. They must know," Fred said. He turned and paced towards the four corners of town, the bright lights illuminating the empty streets. Fred's words hung in the air and I struggled to comprehend his cryptic warning.

"Know what?" I finally managed to stammer.

"That you're new," Fred replied, his tone grave. He pivoted on his heel, his movements sharp against the stillness of the night. "That you're newly dead."

"But . . . I'm not dead," I protested.

Fred continued his brisk pace, his back turned to me as he forged ahead. "You'd better stick with me, otherwise they'll come after ya."

I scampered along behind him as he hurriedly paced toward the four corners. He bore a slight limp which made his steps awkward and labored. He stopped and let me catch up. Once I did, he spoke without turning. "You sound familiar. Did you live in town?" he asked.

"Yes. I live . . . or lived on Bridge Street."
"OK, OK." He rounded the corner and headed into the dimly lit pub. The scent of stale beer and cigarette smoke wafted through the air, mingling with the low murmur of conversation.

At the entrance, Fred paused, his eyes scanning the patrons along the bar. Once he made eye contact with one of them, he stepped closer, his demeanor tentative. "Hey, pal. Got an extra cigarette?"

The patron, a burly man with a weathered face, studied Fred up and down before responding gruffly, "No, man. I don't, sorry."

"OK, OK," Fred muttered, undeterred, and moved on to the next person. "Hey, pal. You gotta . . ."

But before he could finish his request, Big Al's booming voice interrupted. "Come on, Freddie," he interjected.

The bartender circled the end of the bar, shuffling his large body toward the entrance, his large gut proceeding him as he did. "Here." He dug his large, thick hand into his back pocket to produce a pack of cigarettes, pulling out two. "Put one in your ear for later and just," he said with a chuckle, searching his front pocket, and producing a lighter. He held it out to Fred. ". . . enjoy this one for now."

Fred's eyes lit up with gratitude as he took the cigarette between his dry, cracked lips, aiming its end at the flame.

"Thanks, Al. You're good people. You're good people, Al."

Fred bowed, nodded politely, and exited the pub, the door swinging right through me as I followed. He continued towards the bridge, but I froze upon hearing hissing off in the distance.

"Come on," Fred said, coaxing me to follow. "What's your name?" He took many quick puffs as if to savor every last bit of nicotine while still keeping his quick pace.

"Jimmy."

He turned towards me suddenly, his expression guarded. "So," he started, his voice trailing off. ". . . you don't recognize me? I never approached you for a cigarette when you were alive?"

"I'm not dead," I insisted, but he didn't seem convinced. After a moment of silence, I acknowledged, "Yes. You did."

While facing me squarely, he asked, "And? What did you say?" he pressed.

When I studied the man's tanned, leathery, unshaven face, I did as I would have done in the past: I judged him. What was bothersome was—he knew it. But he didn't balk. He maintained his stance as if he were in front of me while still in my embodied state. He continued to the point where I felt uncomfortable, a strange emotion for a bodiless soul. I couldn't help but move away.

"Come on," he crossed the street. Once on the other side,

he stood erect, staring at the taillights of a car that sped by, then maneuvered himself down the embankment, crouching, and leading me underneath the bridge, where there were pieces of a large wooden crate covered with cardboard. Inside was a pillow and blankets. The area was littered with food packaging, pop cans, and cigarette butts.

"What is this?" I inquired.

"This is where I live," Fred replied nonchalantly.

"Here? This . . . this is where you live?"

"It's all I need."

"Why do you say that?"

I couldn't discern his expression in the dim light. As he took a drag from his cigarette, the ember glowed brighter. With a long exhale, he responded, "How much do *you* need?"

"What do you mean?"

"How much do you need . . . now that you're a wandering spirit?"

"I guess I don't need anything . . . material," I responded, contemplating the implications of my newfound state.

Fred took another drag from his cigarette, the glow illuminating his face momentarily. "No. I didn't think so," he remarked, exhaling a plume of smoke. "You and I are no different now, are we?"

"No. I guess not."

"You know . . ." Fred paused to take another drag before flicking his cigarette into the river bank. "Someone once said, 'You can judge the character of a man by how he treats those who can do nothing for him,' or something like that."

I didn't respond.

"That's why I ask for cigarettes. I know I have nothing to offer," Fred continued. He cleared his throat and spat into the rocks beside him. "You don't think I take notice of people's reaction when I ask?"

I remained silent, unable to meet Fred's gaze, consumed by shame for the person I once was when we first crossed paths.

"Anyway," Fred continued, settling his head on the pillow, his face barely illuminated by the soft glow of the street lights reflecting off the river's silvery surface. "You'd better stay close. They won't bother you with me around."

Chapter 6: Jimmy's Body and Billy Gibson's Soul

Wednesday, September 8, 1982 -- 6:45 pm

"Man, that was strange," Jimmy said as he brought his bike down into the basement. He rubbed his right arm with his left hand once again as if to soothe it, but it wasn't painful. That's what he found odd. That upper part of his arm tingled from the sensation he felt while contemplating turning onto gHost Road.

Everything had been strange since he woke that morning. He felt a vibrant rush soon after he woke, and an energy he'd never experienced before. Furthermore, he hadn't sensed his old soul's arrogant, imperious ways. *Is he gone? I don't hear that voice talking at me anymore. Something must have happened last night.*

"Maybe he's gone for good! Good riddance!"

Friday, September 10, 1982 -- 9:07 am

"Jimmy," Mr. Vanderheyden called out, his tone stern, as the young man sheepishly slipped by his boss's office.

"Yes, sir," Jimmy responded, stopping in his tracks and glancing back at his boss.

"You're late. You're never late."

"Sorry, Mr. Vanderheyden. It won't happen again," Jimmy turned to make his way to his desk. However, he was halted once more by his boss's command.

"Come in a minute. Shut the door behind you," Mr. Vanderheyden instructed.

Jimmy complied silently, taking a seat across from the stern man, feeling a knot of apprehension forming in his stomach.

His boss tilted his head slightly before speaking, "I must say. . ." He tapped his finger three times on his desk, causing Jimmy's eyes to follow the movement. "You don't seem yourself lately. I mean . . . you were a zombie, sitting in your chair last week and we had to send you home. Now," he paused. ". . . you're everybody's best friend." He bopped his head as he seemed to agree with himself. "I don't think I need to tell you, you weren't exactly the friendliest chap around here, but . . ." his boss pounded his forefinger on his desk in one firm motion of emphasis. ". . . you get the job done! That's what matters to me."

Jimmy sat perplexed by the news and responded with, "People don't think I'm friendly?"

"You're Mr. Friendly now," Mr. Vanderheyden remarked sarcastically, scowling as if irritated by the interruption. "But that's not the point. Now you show up over an hour late. Gallagher's been waiting at the border for three hours."

Jimmy leaned forward. "Three hours?"

"Yes. Three goddamned hours," Mr. Vanderheyden confirmed, his frustration palpable. "He wasn't cleared last night before you left. Darren had to do that this morning, and we're still waiting, thanks to you."

The staunch middle-aged man's expression grew even more severe, his eyebrows furrowing deeply. He lifted his fat finger, pointing it accusingly at Jimmy. "I'm warning you. I won't put up with any more of this. You got it?"

"Yes, sir," Jimmy replied meekly.

* * *

"Psst," Darren whispered, leaning in to face his troubled co-worker. "What did J.J. want?"

"Who?" Jimmy responded, wrinkling his forehead in confusion.

"Didn't you ever read Spider-Man comics when you were a kid? J. Jonah Jameson. The guy who runs The Daily Bugle. Spider-Man's boss."

"Oh yeah," Jimmy smiled, the memory resurfacing. "You're right. He kind of reminds me of him."

"What did he want?" Darren pressed.

"Gave me shit for being late," Jimmy admitted sheepishly.

"What? You're never late. Jeez," Darren exclaimed.

"Sorry about last night. I guess it slipped my mind."

"Don't worry about it. You've covered for me before and never said anything to J.J. over there," Darren reassured him, gesturing with his thumb towards Mr. Vanderheyden's office.

Jimmy grinned once again, a sense of understanding dawning on him. "I never knew what you meant when you guys would say J.J. Now I know."

"Well, you hadn't exactly been the friendliest of guys," Darren chuckled.

"Yeah," Jimmy mused, reflecting on the events of the past few days. "I've... I've changed, I think," he admitted. He paused, considering his words carefully. "For the better."

10:30 pm

Jimmy knew something was different with his behavior. He wasn't certain he took on another man's soul but realized something good had taken place. If he did have a new soul, it didn't talk to him like his old one did. The absence of the constant chatter from his former soul was welcome.

While lying in bed, Jimmy relished the tranquility of the evening. However, amidst the calm, a nagging thought took root. *That man on the corner of Simcoe and Aylmer Street in Peterborough—he had something for me.* The notion tugged at him, compelling him to return and meet the mysterious figure.

Chapter 7: Jimmy's Soul

Friday, September 10 -- 1982, 9:45 pm

The sun had dipped below the horizon two hours earlier, leaving me alone without Fred, my guardian. I couldn't shake a growing sense of unease. Though the haunting hiss hadn't yet pierced the air, I knew it was imminent. Seeking solace, I hovered beneath the stark glow of the streetlamps at the intersection of Front and Bridge Street.

There! There it is. It was that smoky, snake-like wispy creature accompanied by that disturbing hiss. It shifted forward, then disappeared, followed by the crescendo of a sinister whisper that swung through the air, its deceptive low vibration echoing from building to building, causing me to guess where it was coming from. The sound originated from where the bank stood and then bounced across the building behind me. The reverberation continued toward the dam. Its snake-like hiss grew louder, so I proceeded around the corner and east on Front Street towards the water tower and into the little brick house where I had encountered Beatrice a week earlier. I hated doing it but I was beyond frightened.

I moved to the kitchen; realizing no one was there, I entered the basement, which was pitch black. *No. This is bad. Get up to where she is. I need human protection.* I drifted up both flights of stairs to the bedroom where she was fast asleep, her husband lying beside her.

"Beatrice," I whispered low.

I waited by the bed, peering out at the dimly lit window that shone a low glow onto her face. The hissing had ceased for the moment.

Whispering "Beatrice" once more, I observed the delicate fluttering of her eyelids, signaling her gradual return to consciousness.

With a gentle rustle, she roused from her slumber, "Who's there?"

She rose and sat up, swinging her skinny legs around before reaching for her cane. Walter remained undisturbed, lost in the depths of his dreams.

"Jimmy?" she queried softly.

"Yes," I responded.

"Come." She pushed herself off the bed. Following her lead, I trailed behind as she donned her housecoat. As we descended to the kitchen, she gripped the handrail to provide stability.

"You're in trouble, aren't you?"

"Yes."

"Tell me what happened," she said and reached in the cupboard for a glass, filling it with water. She guided herself to the living room and took her seat in a large padded chair, a neatly folded quilt placed over the top of it. She reached for her sunglasses, placing them over her non-functioning eyes. She lifted her head before saying, "Go on. Tell me what happened."

* * *

I explained to her all that had taken place on gHost Road and the days leading up to Jimmy's body taking in his new soul. She sat perfectly still, her hands folded in front of her. She remained silent, facing me. I wasn't sure if she was processing my story or thinking of how to respond, but her next move surprised me. She groped for her cane, fumbling with it at first. She stood and shifted herself towards the front window, turning her left ear to it.

"They're out there," she said in a low voice. "I can hear them. It's been a while, but I hear them." She wandered to the kitchen, where she dumped the remainder of her water in the sink and bent down to open the bottom cupboard door.

"Come. You can help me," Beatrice urged. As I moved closer, I observed as her fingertips bounced along the array of liquor bottles.

"Which one's the bourbon? This one?"

"No, that's vodka. It's the... yeah. That one."

A sigh escaped her lips as she acknowledged her misstep, "Oh, dear," her frustration evident. "Walter helps me with these kinds of things," she said raising the bottle to the counter, followed by her uncorking it, and pouring a good large splash of it into her cup, which she downed before navigating herself up the stairs, stopping once up.

"Stay with me until morning," she whispered softly before disappearing into her room. I obediently approached her bedside, watching as she settled herself onto the edge of the bed, her small frame sinking into the mattress. With deliberate movements, she lifted her legs onto the bed and enveloped them with the folds of her housecoat, seeking warmth and comfort in its familiar embrace. She lovingly reached out her hand.

I never could understand exactly how humans were able to drive away demon spirits, but it worked. I didn't rest or doze off as I could in my embodied state. I hovered beside Beatrice's bed, listening to the disturbing hissing that would grow and then fade from outside her bedroom window.

Saturday, September 11, 1982 -- 3:01 am
I had gotten used to the patterns of the couple's breaths, which I focused on in hopes of tuning out the frightening sounds of the evil spirits outside the bedroom window. But the wispy-breathy sounds in the room changed. The

low hum I heard in between Beatrice's quiet exhales stopped, causing me to peer up above the edge of the bed.

Walter was sitting up, staring at me. After a moment, he brought his finger to his lips, not saying a word. The old man shifted his position, placing his arm over his wife's midsection and onto her arm. While I observed the two, Walter snuggled up against his wife, she, in turn, shifted herself towards him.

Moments later, I witnessed Walter's spirit leave his body. It was peaceful as it hovered above his body briefly before drifting away, leaving poor Beatrice by herself. That's when I felt it: the pull, a pull that could best be described as a relapse into an addiction; in this case, the desire for a body.

I gazed at Walter's soulless body. The warmth of it now a stark contrast to the chill in the room. *Should I act?* Before I could dwell on the decision, the luminous smoke-like figure I had glimpsed earlier materialized once more, slipping through the walls like a wisp of cigarette smoke. The dreadful hiss echoed through the air.

There's no time to hesitate. It's now or never.

The experience of entering Walter's body could be best described as sticking a hand into a warm empty glove. The basic material served a purpose but it was hollow, void of any humanistic abilities until filled and used for its intended purpose. Although it made for an easy entrance, the transition was odd. The physicality of it was slightly uncomfortable at first, comparable to stepping into someone else's clothes. As I tentatively extended my new limbs, tiny jolts of energy surged through them, like faint electronic pulses coursing through a circuit. Each sensation felt both foreign and exhilarating, as if awakening from a deep slumber. I distinctly remember the sharp tingling that danced along my arm, traveling down to my fingertips, leaving behind a lingering numbing sensation akin to the temporary numbness after my hands were exposed to the frigid Canadian winter air.

But then came the warmth, the body heat, hers nestled up against mine. I remained still, my arm wrapped around the woman who had taken me in, who protected me from the demon spirit. It wasn't just about reclaiming my humanity; it was about connecting with another human being in a profound way. The warmth of human touch, the empathy exchanged in a simple gesture - it was an experience unlike any other. The flood of emotions that washed over me was indescribable, a mix of gratitude, relief, and an overwhelming sense of belonging. I opened my eyes for a moment but didn't move my head as I dared not interrupt this wonderful feeling. A tear fell onto the pillow before closing my lids again. I was truly happy, even though I was now in an elderly man's body.

6:45 am

Although excited to be reacquainted with life in a human physical form, I was incredibly exhausted from the process and had fallen asleep, waking to find that my new companion had left the bed.

"Beatrice?" I called.

My voice. I have a voice. It isn't Jimmy's. It's Walter's.

"Beatrice?" I repeated, with greater volume.

As I rose from the bed, a sharp twinge shot through my lower back, prompting me to instinctively place my hand on the source of discomfort. "Ooh, that hurts," I muttered under my breath, wincing at the sudden pain.

"Walter? Do you need help?" came a voice from downstairs, muffled but concerned.

"No, I'm fine. I think," I replied.

Blinking to clear my vision, I glanced around the room, the details still blurry. *Ah, yes. He wore glasses.* I searched the bedside table for Walter's bifocals, placed them on, and shuffled around the bed with the intent of heading downstairs to greet Beatrice, but the need to relieve myself took over. When I entered the bathroom, I studied my face, my new face; it was long and tired. Walter, now I, had bushy eyebrows and blue eyes that were vibrant and ageless; however, they were almost covered by folds of skin. My messy gray hair looked coarse and wiry. I glanced down at my hands, noting the prominent bluish veins and liver spots that adorned them, a stark reminder of the passage of time.

"Look at you! You're human again," I exclaimed with a grin, marveling at the unfamiliar face that stared back at me from the mirror.

After a moment of self-reflection, I waved to my reflection, chuckling at the novelty of it all, before proceeding to attend to my needs.

With each step down the stairs, I moved cautiously, feeling the weight of my restored humanity, my joints protesting with faint creaks with each movement. When I arrived, Beatrice was lingering at the front living room window, pushing open the left drape.

"Who were you talking to?" she inquired, allowing the drape to fall and turning her attention towards me. As she approached, she tilted her head, expecting a morning kiss.

"Just... greeting myself in the morning. Happy to be alive, I guess," I replied, feeling her hand press against my chest as if to confirm my presence.

"You..." she paused, still pressing lightly. "You were in a mood last night."

"How so?" I inquired, curious about her observation.

"You just... you were frisky. I hadn't seen that side of you in a while. I quite enjoyed it," she remarked with a grin. "You slept in, too. That's not like you."

She settled into her seat, the same spot she occupied the night before when I was without a body. Taking the seat opposite her, I rubbed my arms to chase away the lingering chill of the morning air.

"I'm cold," I confessed.

"Did you forget your housecoat?" Beatrice leaned forward. "Let me fetch it."

"No, no. I'll get it," I insisted, attempting to rise from my seat.

"Nonsense," she declared, rising from her chair and disappearing into the kitchen. "You're an old man. I'm still younger than you, remember?"

As I waited, I couldn't help but feel the ache in my lower back and the coldness creeping into my limbs. I reminded myself that it had only been hours since I was disembodied, so I really couldn't complain.

After a few minutes, Beatrice returned, holding up my housecoat. "Stand up," she commanded, her cane resting by her side. She held open the garment toward me. "Turn around, silly. What's with you? You're like a child. Good Heavens."

I rotated and she placed the housecoat over my shoulders and I re-took my seat.

"Phew! I'm pooped," Beatrice replied, plopping herself on her chair.

I watched as her frail chest heaved and caved as she breathed. She wasn't a small woman, but at first glance appeared weak and tired. Maybe it was the daylight, but it was also the first time I noticed her brightly dyed red hair. It also occurred to me that I had seen her once before, but from where?

"There's tea in the pot. I wasn't sure when you were going to wake up," Beatrice informed me, her voice gentle.

"OK," I replied, preparing to rise from my seat.

"I'll get it. Just... let me catch my breath. You can help me get dressed later."

1:00 pm
After lunch, the two of us sat in the living room while I read the newspaper out loud and Beatrice listened. I wasn't used to wearing glasses, and tilting my head to peer down through the bottom of those bifocals took some getting used to, but it was the only way I could occupy the time.

"Walter?" Beatrice's voice pulled me from my thoughts.

"Yes?" I lifted my head to look at her.

"I have something to tell you," she began, her expression serious.

I placed the paper face down on my lap, ready to listen.
"I had a strange thing happen to me last night," she continued.

"Oh?"

"That spirit. That lost soul who visited us at my séance a couple of weeks ago," she explained, her tone hesitant. "He came to me again last night. He was in danger."

"What do you mean?"

"He asked for protection. Perhaps I shouldn't say this, but... he stayed near me through the night," she confessed.

"In our room?"

"Yes. Poor thing. I hope he's okay. He was gone when I woke."

I reassured her, "I'm sure he's still around."

"I do hope so," she sighed. The room fell into a contemplative silence, broken only by the faint hum of the refrigerator in the kitchen.

I have to admit, the afternoon dragged on. It was incredibly boring. Reading *The Picture of Dorian Gray* probably wasn't the best choice, but it got me through the day. Beatrice loved her husband dearly, that was evident; it made the decision of when and how to tell her the truth increasingly difficult. I knew I couldn't keep the secret long; I needed human form. I wanted it. I desired it, even if I did take on the form of a man in his early eighties. Yes, I checked Walter's wallet. He was eighty-one and his wife, seventy. I felt incredibly aged. My energy was drained, completely sapped. I longed to step outside, to feel the breeze on my face, but my body refused to cooperate. I gave in. *Why didn't I listen to Jimmy when I was in his body?* I wondered.

Chapter 8: Jimmy's Body and Billy Gibson's Soul

Saturday, September 11, 1982 -- 2:30 pm

He didn't take it. No, he didn't snort it when he got home Friday night. He left the cocaine, that he purchased, in that dirty little yellow envelope, stuffed under his socks in the dresser drawer beside his bed—it was calling him though.

"Why now?" he asked himself while sitting perfectly still on his living room couch. "I was going to take it tonight. Can it not wait?"

He stood, then paced his living room, glancing out at the large window, where the view of the row of houses across the street was brightly lit by the early afternoon sun creating a silhouette of the pigeons perched on the roof peaks.

"It's so warm out for September," he muttered, gazing out the window. "I should just . . . get on my bike and go."

He continued pacing the room, his movements restless, scratching his forearms absentmindedly.

"Why am I so nervous about a little coke?" His voice was laced with frustration as he spoke to himself. "Big deal. One snort!"

* * *

"My God. This feels great!" He sped on down Bridge Street, enjoying the sensation of every nerve in his body tingling with pleasure. It was heavenly turning onto Front Street and finally leaving the tiny town, especially the thought of that second floor of that dank apartment above the Fish and Chips restaurant. *No. You won't think about that, he told himself firmly. You'll embrace the beauty of what nature has in store for you.*

He set his sights on the hill ahead, determined. Surprisingly, he barely struggled to climb it, each step carrying him closer to the top. When he finally made it, he felt an overwhelming sense of freedom. The tension melted away, replaced by a wide grin that stretched across his face.

As he descended to the other side, he felt like he was flying. The wind whipped through his hair and the world rushed past in a blur. He zoomed by two horses grazing majestically, their sleek coats shining in the sunlight.

Speeding past the park, he caught glimpses of children laughing and playing, their joy infectious. The sight stirred something deep inside him, a mix of nostalgia and happiness that filled his heart.

He knew he reached his destination, gHost road, because

of the still undisturbed pile of horse dung that was situated in front of the dirt road. When he took a step towards the road, he stopped upon hearing a noise.

"Hey, you!" a man's gravelly voice called from behind him. Jimmy whipped around, searching for the source, but saw no one. The street was empty, the silence unnerving. Confused, he turned back toward gHost road, placing his foot on the pedal, ready to push off.

"Hey, you!" the voice repeated, more insistent this time. "Down here."

Jimmy hesitated, his curiosity piqued. He moved toward the large pile of horse excrement. Kneeling down, he leaned in closer to get a better view of the dried-up clump, feeling ridiculous yet intrigued.

"You speak?" he whispered, a mix of disbelief and wonder coloring his voice.

"Of course, I do." The layers of dung moved as it spoke, resembling that of a large brown sock, moving in the same way it would if you could stick your hand in it to make a sock-puppet.

"Well, isn't that something? You can…" Jimmy began, his eyes wide with shock, but a truck roared by, drowning out his words.

"That's right. I need to warn you," the gravelly voice continued as the noise faded.

"Warn me?" Jimmy pulled his head back, confusion and a flicker of fear in his eyes. "Warn me of what?"

"What do you think? Leaving your soul behind. Abandoning it as if it was a car that won't start anymore."

"So? What of it?" he answered firmly, trying to keep his voice steady.

"Oh, I know what you did. You took on another's. You took on Billy Gibson's soul without even giving it any consideration," the voice accused.

Jimmy's mind raced, memories and guilt flooding back as he struggled to find words. This confirmed what he had been feeling all along. Billy was vibrant and peaceful. He was likable. *That's why everyone started liking me at work. It wasn't only because my old soul was gone, it was because Billy had taken over. It all makes sense now.*

"Sure," the pile continued, its tone almost mocking. "It was wonderful at first, wasn't it? The rush, the freedom, the novelty of a new life."

Jimmy's breath caught in his throat. He remembered those initial days, the euphoria of a fresh start.

"But then... something happened," the voice went on, more serious now. "Your new soul fell back into its addictive behavior, the very habits it never sorted out before its body perished."

Jimmy felt a cold wave of realization wash over him. He had noticed the urges creeping back, the old cravings he thought he'd left behind. His heart sank as he knelt there, the gravity of his actions hitting him harder than ever. Jimmy ignored the fact that Billy's soul came with a few shackles.

"I know who you are, but no one else will. You've lost your identity," the voice declared, a note of finality in its tone.

"What do you mean?" Jimmy's voice trembled, the enormity of the accusation gnawing at him.

"Do you not understand the English language? You're a fake. You're a fraud! You're nothing but a hunk of flesh with a replaced circuit board, floating around the outskirts of a small town that barely knew you existed in the first place." The words hit Jimmy like a slap to the face. "As for your ex-soul, he was selfish, self-centered, and shallow. I pity anyone who would go into the afterlife with a soul like his."

Jimmy's mind reeled. "You mean my old soul? It's dead?" He asked, desperation creeping into his voice.

"Almost. He's had his tough lessons too, you know. I believe he's learned from this. And you, with this... replacement. It won't end well." The voice softened slightly, almost sounding compassionate. "You need to reunite with your original soul before it's too late."

"What do you mean... before it's too late?"

"You haven't a clue, have you?"

"I..." Jimmy paused, bracing himself for another harsh critique from the pile of dung. "No. I guess I don't."

"Don't worry. I figured that out already." The pile remained motionless, the anticipation building in Jimmy's chest as he waited for its response. "Your old soul. Your *real* soul is in danger. It is still amongst us, still in this small town, wandering aimlessly. It gave up on you when you acquired your fake one."

"It gave up?" Jimmy's voice cracked.

"Shut it! Let me finish." The voice snapped. "There are evil spirits that linger. They're everywhere, in every town, in every corner of the world where humans live, scavenging for bodiless souls such as his. Luckily for him, some kind soul, or should I say souls, have protected him. They exist, you know, kind souls."

Jimmy's mind raced, trying to grasp the gravity of the situation. "What do I do?"

"You need to re-enter that house and rid yourself of the one you hold. His body has expired. His mother has not accepted that he is dead. It is unfair to her. She needs to begin mourning and lay him to rest, to soothe her mind. You are torturing her by housing his soul."

"Seriously? Is that my purpose? To muddle through life with my original one?"

"Purpose? Oh, I see. You don't understand what your role is, do you?" The voice sounded almost amused.

Jimmy shrugged his shoulders, feeling a mix of helplessness and irritation. "No, I guess I don't."

"Why am I not surprised." The pile paused, as if gathering its thoughts before continuing. "You see, for me, I serve my purpose. In time, a strong downpour will wash me from the roadside, and after several more, I'll fertilize the grass that's been blessed with my presence."

Jimmy listened, the absurdity of the situation not lost on him, yet the words held a strange wisdom.

"As for you humans, it's not so simple. You are a complicated creature. For instance, when you die, you place your fellow beings in a wooden box or set their carcass on fire; their flesh is no longer given back to the earth. Furthermore, your nutrients are not returned to it or taken in by other species. If anything, you pollute this planet and give nothing in return."

Jimmy's eyes widened, the harsh truth of the words hitting him hard.

"So, my criticism of you being a taker and not a giver is not only against you personally; no, I apply it to the entire human species." The voice grew solemn, as if imparting a final lesson.

Jimmy scanned the farmers' fields, but he couldn't form a response. He simply took it in.

"Hey, you!"

"Yes. I'm still here."

"So, since you humans have little to give to this precious earth, you must at least give to your fellow creature. And I don't mean just friends and family; I mean all of humanity, starting with those in this little town. Therefore, be kind to your fellow human, and most importantly, be accepting of the soul you were born with. That's your purpose."

A large blue Pontiac sped by, stirring up a cloud of dust that made Jimmy cough and squint against the grit.

"What... what happens if I don't make it in time? What happens to me? What happens to my old soul?" he asked.

"Extreme loneliness."

"For who?" he prodded, turning to study a farm tractor laboring toward them. Jimmy stepped aside to let it pass. "For..." the voice continued, but was abruptly cut off as the tractor's large rear wheel squished the mass of horse feces, disfiguring it and leaving tread marks throughout.

Jimmy knelt towards the mangled pile, desperation in his eyes. "For?"

The pile didn't respond.

After a few minutes of waiting, he stood, pondering what to do next, scanning the now vacant paved road and then on to the dirt one that led to the abandoned farmhouse. Without further thought, he pushed himself off with his left foot and cycled along the dirt road, the sun beaming down on him.

The Holstein cows that were huddled along the fence scattered and trotted to the other side of the field. Once at the house, he laid his bike on the gravel and checked his watch, which read 3:30 pm. Placing his hand on the doorknob, he hesitated before turning it. It creaked loudly before banging against the inside of the wall. The musty odor was almost overpowering.

Peering up at the staircase, he placed his hand on the banister, taking his first step, making a loud creak, stopping his movement in anticipation of something stirring up top; nothing did. He continued up the stairs, each step creaking ominously under his weight. The next step popped, as though it was going to give way. He took a deep breath, then a few more, trying to steady his racing heart. About halfway up, he felt his blood pressure change and a wave of dizziness. Once on the second floor, he hung onto the banister to steady himself.

"Phew!" he exhaled, relief mingling with exhaustion. That's when he saw the window, that fantastic window that had always captivated him. But it wasn't as sunny as it had been just a moment before. The light seemed dimmer, casting long shadows across the floor. He approached it cautiously, a sense of unease creeping in.

Jimmy scanned his watch, which had stopped. He tapped it, but the second hand wouldn't move. He re-focused his attention on the window, moving closer. It was dark and not a midnight black, but a sinister darkness; it was hauntingly lifeless. The scenery was unlike anything he'd seen before. Any vegetation was either dead or in the process of dying, specifically one mass; its long roots were so entangled that it twisted and turned, choking itself in the process; its colors were brownish gray, producing even darker shadows.

"What is that?" Jimmy whispered, his voice trembling.

Something emerged from the ink-black scenery beyond the window. A face. A ghostly, emaciated face with its mouth opening and closing, calling out. Its voice was faint at first, barely audible.

"What?" Jimmy called out across the window pane.

"Down the hall," the apparition called with an unnatural whisper.

He turned his attention to the landing, his breath quickening. "There. I can hear it," he muttered to himself. He made careful steps, navigating around the hole in the floor, his pulse racing as he paced toward the long hallway that led to a darkened bathroom. The air grew colder, heavier, with each step he took.

"Come," it called again, the voice eerily familiar.

Jimmy's heart skipped a beat. *I know that voice*, he thought. A figure lay in a tub in the bathroom, lit only by the slit of light penetrating from the perimeter of the window's blinds. That's when he heard it, the arrhythmic drip of water into a larger body of it. The sound echoed through the silent house, changing with the volume of each drop.

"Where are you?" Jimmy called out, his voice echoing off the walls.

"I'm here," came the reply, faint but unmistakable.

"Billy?" Jimmy's throat felt dry as he spoke. "Is that you?"

"Stay there," Billy's voice was firm, commanding. "Don't come any closer."

Jimmy remained rooted to the spot.

"Sit," Billy instructed. "Sit over there. Across from me."

Jimmy obeyed, lowering himself onto the cool, damp bathroom floor. The silence stretched between them, broken only by the steady drip of water every five to seven seconds.

"What is that?" Jimmy finally asked.

"What is what, my friend?" Billy's voice was calm, almost serene.

"That noise. That dripping sound."

"Shhhh," Billy hushed him.

It was shortly after being shushed by Billy Gibson's former self that Jimmy felt a strange sensation. A warmth spread through his cold rump and legs, tingling and comforting at the same time.

"It's kicking in now, isn't it?" Billy's voice echoed in the dimly lit bathroom.

Jimmy opened his mouth to speak, but all that came out was a line of drool, dribbling down his chin. He awkwardly wiped it away before dropping his hand to the floor with a dull clunk.

"It's OK to be dead... isn't it, Jimmy?"

Jimmy nodded weakly, his eyelids flickering before finally shutting.

"Maybe the pile of shit was right. Maybe I should leave you," Billy mused aloud, his voice heavy with resignation. But Jimmy remained motionless and unresponsive, lost in a world between life and death.

When Jimmy opened his eyes, he found himself on the steps to the farmhouse, rubbing his face, then peering up to view the afternoon sun.

"How did I end up down here? I thought I was..." He swung around to see the door to the abandoned farmhouse closed, the screen door hanging by its hinges, swaying slightly in the breeze. Confusion and disorientation clouded his mind as he contemplated what to do next.

"Ah, this is nice," he murmured, a fleeting moment of peace washing over him. With a heavy sigh, he closed his eyes and stretched his neck out, allowing the warm sunlight to bathe his face.

He embraced the warmth of the rays on his cool skin, and the calmness of the pleasant outdoors. He was able to tune out the noises and twisted images in his head, which was wonderful for the few minutes it lasted. But his moment of euphoria was broken by a constant flutter that was evident from the other side of his eyelids. When he opened them, he discovered that he was surrounded by starlings, a common bird he'd seen so many times on the front lawn of his house. There were dozens upon dozens of them. They surrounded him, pecking alongside his legs and buttocks.

"Are they... pecking at me? There's nothing here to..." Jimmy's voice faltered as he struggled to comprehend the strange sensation.

Before he could finish his thought, he noticed hordes of tiny white worms inching their way along the steps beside him. Hundreds and hundreds of them wriggled in a relentless, undulating mass, working their way along one step before tumbling onto the next. The sight was both mesmerizing and horrifying. Jimmy's stomach churned at the grotesque display.

He jumped away from the door and it was only then that he realized the birds weren't pecking at him; they were eating the white maggots that were escaping from under the door frame. He backed away, almost to his dropped bike. Swarms of birds came from everywhere, darting for the steps. The tiny white worms fell from the bottom step onto the soil and squirmed along the grass, barely advancing two or three inches before being gobbled up. What was more horrific was the constant droves of maggots that spilled from under the gap of the door and onto the steps. Flocks of all breeds of birds arrived; woodpeckers, chickadees, goldfinches, and even vultures swooped down, scaring the others away briefly before the smaller species would return. Still eyeing the scene, Jimmy reached for the handlebars of his bike, but immediately dropped it. The chirps and whistles of the birds were briefly interrupted by its crash. He hesitated for a moment before motioning towards the door, placing his foot onto the first step, squishing the worms under the sole of his shoe, and following it with another. Concentrating on his next move, he twisted the door handle and pushed it open wildly. From the opening, came a river of puny worms, crawling and falling over the thickly caked wall that formed when the door had blocked them. The staircase was covered in a white carpet of maggots, descending from above. When he peered down, his shoes were covered in white larvae. Un-phased by it, he stepped forward, placing his hand on the banister.

While he stood still, he was distracted by the sound of drops; not the same dripping he heard previously, but a different noise.

Splat, splat, splat!

Curiosity and unease gnawed at him as he proceeded up the steps, one by one, determined not to lose focus on his mission. The strange noise echoed in his mind, urging him to move faster. His pace quickened until he reached the top. The room spun, causing him to close his eyes. When he reopened them, he studied the parade of worms that branched on the landing and down the stairs, while others fell into the hole and landed on the floor below causing the splatting noise.

He took in a few more breaths before moving toward the end of the hall. *That's where they're coming from—the bathroom.* Jimmy stopped before turning in.

"Billy?" he called out low.

Creeping towards the open door, he finally had the nerve to turn the corner. There, in the dry bathtub was a human skeleton, its flesh completely eaten away by the plethora of maggots.

Jimmy ran down the hall but slipped and fell on the slimy white worms that coated the hardwood floor. Making every attempt to not vomit from the muculent film that remained on the side of his face when it bounced against the carpet of larvae, he pushed himself to his knees, the maggots oozing from between his fingers as he did. Once to his feet, he ran down the stairs, almost slipping again as he fled, until finally out of that house.

* * *

7:00 pm
Jimmy woke in a fetal position while on the couch. After he sat up and peered out the window, he jerked his head to search for his clock.

"Jesus! It's seven." He stood and scanned his torso, trying to piece together his fragmented memories. He peered down to determine how he was dressed; it was the same clothes he had on before taking his line of coke.

"Did I even leave the couch?"

Placing his hand on his forehead, he scanned the room where he stored his cycling shoes. They were untouched.

"No. I didn't even make it out of the living room. God! That was messed up. No way. No more."

Determined, he grabbed the tiny yellow envelope from the side table and tossed it into the garbage bin, snarling at the white powder that was scattered among the refuse.

Chapter 9: Jimmy's Soul

Tuesday, September 14 -- 1982, 2:00 pm

There was something comforting about being in human form again. I never appreciated it while in Jimmy's body. I had also forgotten how the physical presence of someone could change my outlook. The love and warmth I experienced were undeniably comforting. I was overwhelmed by how much it delighted me. The aches, pains, and low energy didn't matter anymore. Instead of seeing them as a detriment, I realized they were reminders that I was alive. *How often does someone get a second chance in life?*

Lost in my thoughts, I was suddenly jolted back to reality. "I need to call Delores and Agnes," Beatrice blurted out, causing me to jump in my chair.

During the preceding three days, I had become accustomed to Beatrice's habits, one of which was taking naps during the afternoon. She did so with her sunglasses on; therefore, I could never quite tell when she was truly asleep, so moments like this caused a jolt to my carriage.

"Who?" I asked.

She sat up and "stared", from behind her sunglasses. She even sniffed the air between us, pausing for a moment before leaning back in her chair. I immediately realized my blunder but couldn't think of a quick way to cover it up.

"My book is..." She raised her hand and continuously patted the table beside her, searching for and finally discovering her small telephone book. She gripped it and passed it to me. "Bradly. Delores Bradly. Dial the number for me, please." Her tone had changed to a methodic, almost monotone one, a stark contrast from earlier.

I took the book from her, my fingers trembling slightly as I flipped through the worn pages to find the number. I felt a pang of guilt for my earlier slip-up. As I dialed, I glanced at Beatrice, her expression now calm but distant.

Saturday, September 18, 1982 -- 12:00 am

I sat at the card table with my fingers resting on the planchette. To my left was Dolores Bradly, the tiny woman who had sat next to Walter when I first entered the house. She had short hair that just covered her neck and was combed forward on top. It didn't appear to be colored and was still naturally brown. Everything about her was tiny; her nose, her eyes, her face, her arms, her hands. I found that she didn't make eye contact very often, but when she did, she appeared to be a woman who was a very good judge of character. To my right was Agnes; she was not as tiny, but a short woman with a pale complexion, a pug nose, and for the most part, an expressionless face. She made a "wheezy" sound when she breathed, which was comical at first, but soon became irritating. Her quintessential blue-tinged hair contrasted her bland expression. Although I had difficulty reading her, I found studying her hair a guilty pleasure.

The room was lit by a single candle beside the Ouija board, its flame steady and unwavering, casting eerie shadows on the walls.

"Walter. Your hands are shaking," Beatrice stated, her voice a mixture of concern and authority.

"I can't help it," I replied, my voice trembling.

I was nervous, jittery because Beatrice wanted another séance. I couldn't stop it from happening, but I was worried about the results. *Will I rise out of Walter's body? Will other spirits come?* It was difficult for me to relax, but I tried to remain calm to avoid raising suspicion.

"Close your eyes, everyone," Delores instructed, her voice squeaky and meek, breaking the tense silence. I took a deep breath and closed my eyes, feeling the weight of anticipation in the room. My hands, still trembling, rested on the planchette as I braced myself for whatever might come next. I was frightened. Although I had been a wandering spirit before, I found the situation unnerving, perhaps because I was too comfortable in my new skin, my new carriage, my new body from which I was frightened of being evicted. The thought of it brought back all those lonesome moments I had while shifting through this town without a friend. All the memories of gHost Road returned; the one hour and seven-minute delay, the separation from Jimmy. *Could it happen again? Could it happen tonight?*

I heard Beatrice take in a breath before speaking, "Speak to us, oh kind spirit. This is Beatrice. I know you are amongst us. Come to me. Speak to me, kind spirit."

From beyond my eyelids, I noticed the orange flame flutter, but I kept my eyes shut. Shortly after, an unrecognizable odor entered the air, faint but unsettling.

"It's here," Beatrice whispered, her voice tinged with a mix of awe and trepidation. "Who are you?"

I felt it. I sensed the movement of the planchette beneath my fingers. The air around us seemed to thicken, charged with an electric tension. I could hear my own heartbeat, each thud echoing in my ears. I fought opening my eyes and succeeded, letting the three of us move with the planchette as Delores took note of where it landed. The tiny heart-shaped piece of wood moved, and I felt it stop at each letter briefly before continuing on to the next. After the final stop, I heard Dolores gasp.

"Bea. It's Walter."

Agnes lifted her hand from the board to cover her mouth. I opened my eyes to discover the tiny notetaker staring at me. I felt like a thief caught by the police with one leg over the window sill. When I peered down at the planchette, I could still feel Delores's piercing gaze.

"Close your eyes, please," she insisted.

I did as the tiny woman asked, my eyelids shutting out the dim light. The room's silence was finally broken by Beatrice.

"Are you at peace, darling?" Beatrice's voice was soft, almost tender.

The planchette moved again.

"Yes," Delores responded, her voice steady.

Beatrice blurted her next question. "Walter, were you forced out of your body?"

The planchette moved. "No," read Delores.

I could hear my companion let out a sigh, but it wasn't one of relief. It was heavy, burdened with unresolved tension.

"Walter, whose soul occupies your body?" Beatrice asked, her voice trembling slightly.

I felt the planchette move five times before Delores answered, "Jimmy."

After what seemed like minutes, Beatrice asked hesitantly, "Is he a good spirit?"

The tiny pointer moved once more.

"Yes."

I could hear another sigh, this time of relief.

With the missed opportunity to tell Beatrice proactively, I suddenly felt ashamed and unwanted, a true imposter; however, I needed to remain calm. My eyes remained closed even though I fought the urge to open them and view the unwelcome glares. Beatrice wasn't finished with the connection to her late husband.

"Walter." Her voice was shaky and broke at the final syllable. "I never got to say goodbye to you." She took a breath. "I know I've never told you, but... I want to say that I've always loved you. I'm sorry I never told you in person."

Agnes sniffled as I continued to press my lids closed.

Beatrice continued, "Do you forgive me? For what I did?"

Struggling with the desire to open my eyes and observe the outcome, I fought against it, anticipation building inside me. Finally, the planchette moved and Delores responded softly, "Yes."

I could hear Agnes's soft sobs, a mixture of relief and lingering sadness.

It was evident that Beatrice and her friend Agnes had difficulty holding their emotions. Dolores, on the other hand, kept cool. A few seconds passed before the silence was overtaken by Bea's voice. "Do you still love me, Walter?"

I could feel my body tense in anticipation of the spirit's answer. The room felt like it was holding its breath. The planchette began to move, slow and deliberate, tracing a path across the board when finally, it swung towards Delores, who responded with a single, heart-wrenching: "Goodbye."

Bea's face crumpled, tears spilling down her cheeks as she let out a small, choked sob. The connection was broken, leaving an icy chill in the room. It was when Beatrice broke down that I finally opened my eyes, witnessing Dolores rubbing her friend's arm, consoling her while her hostess dabbed her eyes from under her glasses.

"He'll reach out again," Agnes said, handing Bea a box of tissues. "Don't worry."

I did what I thought was most appropriate. I stood and angled myself with the intention of going upstairs.

"Where do you think you're going?" called Delores's squeaky voice.

"It's OK, Lola," Beatrice responded with a sniffle. "I know who it is. He's the spirit I met a few weeks ago. You remember, girls, when I approached it. He's a kind soul. A troubled one, mind you."

"What are you going to do with him?" Agnes whispered indiscreetly.

Beatrice sighed and reached her hands out toward her guests. "Thank you for being such lovely friends. But I must get acquainted with this Jimmy fellow."

"No. No," Agnes remarked firmly, her voice carrying a note of determination. "We won't let you be alone with him. Let us determine if he is a good soul or not. Remember, I was a school teacher. I've come across all sorts of characters."

Beatrice appeared torn.

"She's right, Bea," Delores chimed in. "Let us stay until we feel you're safe."

Beatrice nodded slowly, her shoulders sagging with the weight of their collective worry. "Alright," she relented. "But please, let me talk to him. I need to understand."

"May I..." I interjected, raising my hand tentatively. "Explain everything that happened to me?"

Dolores gave me a stern look. "I'd think you'd better."

2:00 am
While I described my situation and my reasoning for taking on Walter's body, Agnes seemed unconvinced. Dolores, on the other hand, appeared more receptive, her

body language open and encouraging, though she leaned slightly on her blind friend for support.

"Are you telling me you're from here, in town?" Agnes pressed.

"Yes," I affirmed, nodding. "You see, my body still exists, much like Walter's does. My former self owns a house on Bridge Street."

Beatrice hadn't said anything after I explained why I entered Walter's body. This silence was finally acknowledged by her tiny friend.

"Bea. Are you OK?" Dolores asked gently.

"I knew almost right away you weren't Walter," Beatrice confessed. "You didn't place your hand on my shoulder when I kissed you. That was something he always did. And you have a sort of sweet odor about you."

I lowered my head. I examined my wrinkled hands, feeling the weight of loneliness settle in once again.

"Do you want me to leave?" I asked.

Bea laughed softly, her exhaustion evident as she let out a breath. "Do you think I'd kick an old man out on the street?" She shook her head gently, a tired smile on her face. "No, no. You will stay." She turned to her friends.

"Ladies, my good ol' girlfriends. Come next weekend for tea."

Agnes looked uncertain, her brows furrowed in concern. "Bea, that's a week away. Are you sure?"

Beatrice waved off her concern with a dismissive hand. "Good heavens, you two. He's slept with me for the last seven nights. I'll need a week with this... new soul. Besides, we'll need the time to make a plan to get this Jimmy back into his own body. And..."

She paused, her voice trailing off as she seemed lost in thought. Dolores leaned forward slightly, her eyes filled with curiosity. "Yes, Bea," she prompted gently.

"Maybe," Beatrice said thoughtfully, bringing her finger to her chin. "Maybe it will allow Walter to return. Perhaps it's not too late."

6:45 am

Once I heard Beatrice wake, I shuffled my achy bones to the kitchen and put the kettle on, placing two Red Rose Tea bags in a pot.

I had offered to sleep on the couch, which I regretted, as my aged frame couldn't stand the lumpy furniture. Because of that, I had been awake since five in the morning. She said that she needed the night alone, which I respected. I was also thankful for not being asked to leave. Even though I had rarely seen her eyes, I determined that I didn't need to. Her warmth towards me, even while a spirit, never wavered. She was still pleasant and caring, just as she was that morning when she descended from the bedroom.

"You're up already?" she asked as she made her final steps, her hand lightly grazing the banister for balance.

"Good morning," I said, standing awkwardly in the kitchen. "The couch was... not so comfortable."

I expected her to pass by me, locate her chair, and take a seat—but she didn't. Instead, she stopped in front of me and tugged gently at the sleeve of my housecoat.

"Tonight, you will sleep in our bed. I don't think I can manage another night alone," she admitted.

A smile spread across my face, one that I wished she could see. But she didn't need to; she seemed to sense it anyway.

"That is..." she continued, her steps slow and deliberate as she moved into the living room. "If you wish to."

4:00 pm
"Jimmy?"

I was startled awake, my eyes snapping open just as I was about to doze off. The voice pulled me back to the present, and I refocused on Beatrice, sitting across from me in the dimly lit living room.

"Yes?" I said, trying to steady my racing heart.

"You can ask me what you've been wanting to."

"I don't know what you mean."

"You've given your confession. Now it's time to give you mine."

"You're talking about..."

"Walter. Yes."

I sat perfectly still, waiting for her to continue.

"It happened years ago." She paused, licking her lips nervously. "I tried to hide it from him. I was successful. In fact, I was successful for twenty-two years." She pushed her red hair to one side with her left hand, her gaze seemingly fixed on the wall across from us.

"Successful in...?" I prompted gently.

"In keeping a secret—of an affair. I had..." She turned to face me. "...and still have a healthy libido."

I shifted uncomfortably in my chair.

"I was in my late thirties and Walter... Walter seemed to have lost interest in me. I loved the man. I *still* love the man. But I needed more. Lord knows I was wrong, but I did what I did. It was selfish of me. I regretted it later," Beatrice quivered, her voice filled with sorrow.

"He's forgiven you," I stated gently.

"Not at first." She shook her head slowly. "When I became blind, that's when he forgave me. He pitied me... and then... well, after some time, he forgave me. It was difficult. Yes, I know I deserved it. It was God's way."

I waited for her to continue, sensing there was more she needed to say.

"Now... now he holds the power again."

"I don't know what you mean," I added.

"The power," she paused, her hands smoothing out the wrinkles in her pants—an obvious nervous tick. "...of the relationship. You know..." She seemed lost in her thoughts for a moment before continuing. "I could do, or say whatever I wanted and Walter would just follow along. Yes." She nodded as if convincing herself. "I could read him like a book. Even when he discovered the infidelity, I still held it."

She made an unusual face, almost like a smirk. Her expression seemed to reflect a mixture of regret and a twisted sense of satisfaction.

"He was a jealous man. Whenever we'd go out to a dance or a party, he would become flustered when a man took a moment to talk to me. My God," she waved her hand in the air, her frustration palpable even in memory. "The most innocent situations would upset him to the point where he would grab my arm and demand we go home." She paused, lost in the recollection. "But then... then it shifted."

She grabbed her cane and leaned forward on it, seemingly replaying a scene in her mind. "It shifted when I became blind. I needed him... yes, I did. I was dependent on him." Her head nodded hesitantly, stopping halfway, then she grinned. "And he knew it. He never rubbed it in my face. It wasn't in him to do that. No, he couldn't hold on to it very long. He told me he forgave me. When he did, that's when the power shifted to me. Do you know what I did?"

She angled her glasses at me.

"I re-took it! I could have left it, but no, I ruined a perfectly balanced marriage. I suppose I was angry, angry at God for punishing me, so I took it out on poor Walter. I never told him that I loved him. I regret that. It was a scheming, selfish way of maintaining my power over the marriage. That's why I asked him if he forgave me. That question last night wasn't referring to the infidelity. He already forgave me for that. It was about me re-taking the power. Perhaps he was OK with it. But... he achieved the power last night." Beatrice grinned, a bittersweet smile. I could see the complexity of emotions playing out on her face—regret and a strange sense of humility. But she wasn't finished with her story.

"Anyway, that's when I gained the gift. Soon after I became blind."

"The gift?" I asked, leaning in, curious.

"When I became blind, well... it happened so quickly; it wasn't similar to any other disease, like glaucoma. I didn't have time to prepare myself for it. I had to learn to manage around the house—and those damned stairs. My goodness. Walter insisted we move, but I was persistent, so we stayed. I didn't want to take him away from our house of nearly thirty years. Anyway." She leaned back in her chair, placed her cane beside her, and then rested her hands on her lap. "I managed. *We* managed."

She paused, her fingers fidgeting with the cuff of her sweater. "I was humbled. It wasn't just the infidelity that weighed on me. You see, Jimmy. I wasn't a very good human being. I was extremely critical of others... of those less fortunate. I remember the Johnston family next door. Yes, sir. Bob Johnston..." She seemed to stare at the west wall again, her eyes distant as if seeing a memory play out. This time, her focus drew me to turn and look too, though there was nothing there.

She poked her finger under her glasses to wipe a tear. "Bob Johnston worked at the tannery. Did his twelve-hour days, all the while his wife drank; the woman was a downright alcoholic. The strength it must have taken him to stay with that woman. Anyway, those kids were always running around, screaming, laughing; their faces were always dirty. I couldn't stand it. I wasn't very pleasant to him or those kids. When I became blind… why… I couldn't see their dirty little faces anymore. You'd think I'd be…" Beatrice broke off her sentence and fished out a tissue that was tucked in the sleeve of her sweater. She dabbed her eyes and nose, the tissue crinkling softly in the quiet room.

"You'd think I'd be happy about that. No. I was sad." She took a moment to recollect a memory. "I remember sitting on the porch, wearing my new sunglasses, and one of the girls—Jenny was her name—called out. She said, 'Mrs. Murphy. My mom says you're blind now. Is that true?' I said 'Yes.' Then she says…" She lifted her chin before finishing. "'Mom says I shouldn't call you Mean Mrs. Murphy anymore.'" Beatrice grinned to herself and nodded. "They were right to call me that."

She paused, her expression growing somber. "One day… that little girl got run over by a car. Right down there on Front Street, near the four corners – the first of July, nineteen-seventy-two. I remember because that was my first indication. My first sign."

She continued, her voice soft and filled with emotion. "I woke in the middle of the night, that night. Even before I did, I heard her call, 'Mrs. Murphy.' She had this sweet little voice. Then I heard it once more. Down the stairs I went. I could feel her energy in the living room. I sensed her whisking around the room, almost playfully, and then... she disappeared into the night. Of course, I told my girlfriends about it and so we agreed to host a séance," she continued. "Jenny and I became friends. So, as the saying goes, there's always a silver lining. I'm a better person now than I was before. I see people for who they really are, a wandering spirit, whatever it may be."

"That's why you were able to meet me?" I asked.

"I've met so many spirits over the past ten years. Yet, some of them truly evil. I understand why you claimed Walter's body."

I lowered my head, the weight of my actions pressing down on me.

"We need to help you find your way back."

Chapter 10: Jimmy's Body and Billy Gibson's Soul

Wednesday, September 22, -- 1982, 10:10 pm

It had been just over a week since his bad experience with the street narcotic. Even though he had no intention of buying more from the same scummy-looking man he bought from previously, his ability to avoid all drugs was failing. There was another supplier that could be contacted at some greasy spoon restaurant at George and Hunter Street.

On his way back from his meeting with the new supplier, Jimmy stopped at the intersection of Front and Bridge, waiting for the light to turn green. As he idled, a troubling thought crossed his mind: *Was that just a bad batch of coke? I must find out!*

He put the car into first gear, cranked the steering wheel, and headed west on Front Street. He drove slowly, his mind racing until he reached the bend where he had to gear down to climb the hill. The two headlights pierced the darkness, but despite the lovely, cool, crisp night, a low mist limited visibility to a mere hundred feet. The mist barely illuminated the edges of the grass along the pavement, adding an eerie feel to the night.

"Dammit!" He slammed on the brakes to avoid a raccoon that darted in front, nearly hitting it. The animal scampered off to the other side of the road. The sudden stop stalled the car.

"Jesus Christ!" he exclaimed, his hand flying to his chest as his heart pounded from the sudden scare. Anxiety surged through him, making his pulse race even faster. In an attempt to calm himself, he reached into his jacket for his wallet. Opening it, he exposed the new packet, a grin spreading across his face as he thought about the white substance entering his bloodstream.

"Maybe now is just as good a time as any," he said to himself.

* * *

Jimmy started the car and left it idling, but his moment of relief was eventually disrupted by a woman's cry and scream, which in turn caused him to roll down his window. *It's coming from . . . there!* Several hundred feet away from the road stood a small house, the square window of its front door glowed from the interior lights. Jimmy exited the car, leaving it running by the side of the road. The night was eerily silent, his breath visible in the cool air.

Suddenly, *Bang!* The main door of the house flew open, slamming against the wall. A figure emerged—a woman, struggling with the screen door handle before finally pushing it open. The glass in the door shattered against the house as she fled into the darkness.

Jimmy stood quietly for a moment, his eyes straining to pierce through the dense fog that had settled around him. He tried to follow the woman's movements but lost sight of her as she disappeared into the thick mist. His heart raced, not from fear but from the adrenaline coursing through him, his curiosity and concern battling within.

"Deborah!" A second figure emerged, his stocky frame nearly blocking the light spilling out from inside the house. His voice was deep and furious. In his hand, he clutched a looped object that swung back and forth ominously. Without hesitation, he bolted from the doorway and vanished into the dark after her.

"Deborah!" His voice echoed against the trailers across the road, the sound carrying through the still night. Jimmy's pulse quickened, anxiety gnawing at him as he stood there, unsure of what to do next. He could feel the tension in the air, the desperation in the man's call, and the fear in the woman's hurried escape. Jimmy spun around to watch some of the porch lights turn on as the sound traveled through the still air. With the car still sputtering, he had difficulty determining where the two had escaped. He took a few steps in front of the car in a creeping motion, so as to not be noticed, scanning the area as he did, viewing only the cool mist swirling in front of his headlights. That's when he jumped.

"Take me, please." Jimmy's eyes popped open, startled by the young woman's fists gripping his jacket. Her face was streaked with tears, her hair disheveled and wild.

"In, in, in," he muttered, fumbling to open the rear door for her. She scrambled inside, and he quickly climbed back into the driver's seat. In his haste, he accelerated too abruptly, causing the car to stall.

"Fuck!" he cursed, frantically restarting the engine.

Just as the car roared back to life, the man ran in front of it, illuminated by the headlights. His husky frame blocked the way; his dark beady eyes glaring directly at Jimmy with arms open wide as if daring him to drive forward.

"Go! He's gonna kill me," the woman in the backseat screamed.

Jimmy didn't hesitate. He slammed on the gas, the car lurching forward. The man flung a belt at the car which slapped against Jimmy's arm through the open window as they sped past.

"You little bitch!" the man yelled after them, his voice growing faint as they gained distance. He shouted something else, but it was lost in the noise of the engine. Jimmy's hands shook on the steering wheel as they drove down the road, the woman sobbing in the backseat. He glanced at her in the rearview mirror.

Jimmy turned onto Asphodel 6th line, accelerating at an incredible speed and stopping only when they arrived at County Road #2. His breaths were short and erratic. When he finally calmed, he turned to the young woman who was sobbing uncontrollably.

"Are you all right?"

With her face still in her hands, she shook her head. Even though he was far away from that house, he felt the need to check his mirrors and his surroundings. He turned onto County Road # 2 and proceeded to drive into the center of town.

"Where am I taking you?" Jimmy asked, his voice tense as he glanced back at the woman in the rearview mirror.

"I don't know," she replied, finally lifting her head from her hands. Her eyes were red and puffy, and her cheeks glistened with fresh tears.

"The police station? Want me to—"

"No!" she hollered, cutting him off abruptly. "That's what started all this."

He didn't respond. While stopped at the red light, he jerked his head west for fear of seeing the intimidating man clambering down Front Street with a belt in his hand. The traffic lights seemed stuck on red forever, so he glanced east to ensure no one was coming before bolting through the intersection and across the bridge until finally turning into his driveway.

Jimmy's mind raced as he tried to make sense of the situation. "You can stay with me until you decide what to do."

The woman nodded, wiping her eyes with the back of her hand.

Deborah sat on the couch while Jimmy boiled the kettle. It allowed her a few minutes to herself while he waited in the kitchen. He grabbed two cups and a tea bag. The kettle cracked and popped, drowning out what his guest had said.

"Sorry." Jimmy peaked around the corner. "I didn't hear you."

She pushed the long strands of her damp brown hair from the side of her red face, exposing her bloodshot eyes. He determined the woman to be in her early twenties.

"I said, thank you for taking me away from him," Deborah repeated. She turned to study her twitchy fingers, her body tense and exhausted.

"May I ask? Who is 'him?'" Jimmy ventured cautiously.

She shook her head, her eyes filling with tears. "I deserved it," she murmured.

"What do you mean?" Jimmy asked, just as the kettle whistled. He moved to shut off the burner, the piercing sound adding to the tension.

"I said nasty things to him," she admitted, her voice breaking. "He's very protective of me, and when I've had too much to drink, I get the courage to lash out. I told him I fucked other men behind his back. That's when he lost it and slapped me." Her words came out in a rush.

She wiped the tears from her eyes, trying to compose herself. "I love him, but I hate it when he's like that." Her chin quivered, and more tears rolled down her cheeks. "I did it. I should have known better. He loves me. I know he does."

Jimmy stood at the doorway to the kitchen, the steam from the kettle curling around him. He couldn't fully grasp the dynamics of what had happened, but he could still see the frightening look on that man's face, something out of a horror movie. The image made him shudder.

He rolled up his sleeve to examine the red mark left on his forearm by the belt. The sight of it brought back the intensity of the moment.

The distraught woman was quiet after they finished their tea. She stared at her cup for a long moment before finally speaking. "Will you drive me to Peterborough tomorrow? I can stay with a friend there," she asked, her voice tentative and hopeful.

"Sure," Jimmy replied, standing up and taking her empty cup. "I'll grab a blanket and pillow for you."

Thursday, September 23, 1982 -- 6:30 am

When his alarm went off, he scanned the cracked ceiling of his bedroom, recounting the prior night's events. He flung off his covers and quickly pulled his jeans over top of his boxers. Just before turning the door handle to his bedroom, Jimmy paused, leaning against the door to listen for any sounds. There was no movement. He twisted the handle and peeked out. The light in the hallway was brighter than usual, causing a surge of panic. He raced to the top of the stairs to find the front wooden door open, the bright morning sun shining through the glass of the screen door.

"Shit!" he muttered under his breath.

He raced downstairs to discover the woman was gone; the blanket was still neatly folded on the couch where he had placed it the night before. "Where the hell would she go?"

Jimmy stood there, perplexed by what had happened over the course of the past eight hours. He was worried for the woman, afraid of the man who might still come after him for rescuing her. The uncertainty gnawed at him, making his stomach churn.

"I'm gonna be late for work."

He dashed back upstairs, quickly stripping off his clothes and jumping into the shower.

* * *

He gulped the last of his coffee and paced toward the dining room table, fetching his jacket. He slipped his arms through it and in a swift movement reached into his right pocket to grab his keys.

"What?" He peered down, then searched in his second pocket. "What the . . . Oh no. Where's my keys?"

He ran out of the house and around to the driveway, only to find a vacant spot where his car normally sat. His heart sank.

"God dammit!" he shouted.

Jimmy crouched down in the middle of the driveway, feeling the weight of the situation pressing down on him like the sky was going to fall. He stayed there for a few seconds, accepting the grim reality that his car was stolen. But then another thought struck him, and he sprang up. "Wait a minute." He yanked his wallet from his jacket pocket, flipping it open. "The money is there. But . . ." He stuck his finger into the wallet, searching for the tiny packet. "For fuck's sake! She took my coke. Shit, shit, shit!"

"Something wrong over there?" his neighbor, Mrs. Austen, called out. She stood in her driveway, holding her purse in front of her, a look of concern on her face.

Embarrassed, Jimmy brought his hand to his forehead, noticing his damp sock-clad feet for the first time. "Nothing, Glenda, I just . . . forgot I took a cab home last night."

"You need a ride somewhere?" she offered, her voice kind but her eyes suspicious.

"No." He turned to head back into the house. "Thank you. I'll call another."

"OK," she responded slowly, still watching him closely.

* * *

"Dammit, dammit, dammit! I try and do a good thing and . . ." Jimmy muttered to himself, as he peeked out the front window, waiting for the cab. "There he is."

Jimmy left the house, a pang of anxiety hitting him as he made a motion to reach for his keys, intending to lock the door behind him.

"Nope. I can't do that either. No house keys, remember?" he said, shaking his head ruefully at his forgetfulness.

"Where to?" the cabbie asked as Jimmy climbed into the backseat.

"1200 Industrial Drive, Peterborough."

The driver shifted the car into reverse, and they pulled away from the curb, heading down Bridge Street. Jimmy glanced out the window, his usual morning routine disrupted by the chaos of the past night. The familiar buildings passed by in a blur, his mind preoccupied with thoughts of Deborah, his missing car, and the mess he found himself in.

8:45 am

"Wait here, please," Jimmy said to the cabbie before dashing up the stairs, his breath coming in short, ragged gasps as he reached his boss's office.

"Mr. Vanderheyden," he panted, trying to catch his breath. "I'm sorry I'm late. My car got stolen last night. I had to take a cab here. Can someone take me to the police station?"

His boss glanced at his watch, his expression a mixture of annoyance and concern.

"The cab is still here," Jimmy added quickly. "I told him to wait."

"Jesus Murphy," Vanderheyden muttered. "I can't afford to have two of ya's gone. Have the driver take you. Call me when you're done," he instructed, turning to the dispatch room before fixing Jimmy with a stern stare. "And I want to see that damned police report when you get back!"

"Yes, sir," Jimmy replied, feeling a knot of tension tightening in his stomach as he turned to leave the office.

5:05 pm

He wasn't himself all day. The prior night's events ran through his mind, over and over. He found it exhausting. His boss was very displeased and wouldn't show empathy. He was treading on thin ice and knew that one more mess-up would get him fired. Darren was kind enough to drive him home that evening after work.

"You know," Darren started, leaning back in his seat, "I think J.J.'s being a bit of a dick. I mean really. It's not your fault your car got stolen."

Jimmy remained silent, his thoughts elsewhere, his gaze fixed on the passing scenery outside the window.

"Are you OK?" Darren pressed, sensing Jimmy's unease.

It was a sudden and strange curiosity that came over Jimmy as soon as the car stopped at the red light at Front and Bridge Street.

"Turn here," Jimmy ordered, interrupting Darren's train of thought.

"Sure. But I thought you lived—"

"I want to check something out. It won't take long."

"OK," Darren replied.

Without explaining the events of the previous night to his coworker, Jimmy directed him to the familiar scene. Jimmy sat up in the car like a child about to arrive at the county fair. He needed to revisit the site where it all happened. Darren's car advanced up the hill slowly as Jimmy peered up. There was one more bend before the vehicle approached the house where he rescued the woman who stole his car. But once the road straightened, Jimmy opened his mouth and was about to tell Darren to slow down, but that's not what came out of his mouth.

"There's a ... what the hell?" Jimmy exclaimed, his voice rising with disbelief.

"Isn't that your..."

"That's my car!" Jimmy interrupted, his heart racing as he recognized the familiar green Saab.

His car was sitting at the same spot where he had picked up the girl the night before.

Jimmy climbed out of his co-worker's car and hovered around his vehicle as if he were staring at a rare piece of art. He opened the door and entered, bending over to search for his keys.

"Oh, yeah . . ." Jimmy sighed upon discovering the open packet of cocaine, the remnants of white powder still on the passenger's seat.

He grabbed the yellow packet and tucked it under the seat before exiting the vehicle and returning to his co-worker's car.

"It's my car alright. The keys are missing, though."

"How did you know it was here?" Darren inquired.

Jimmy sighed heavily before responding, "It's a long story."

"Seriously. Is everything okay? You haven't been yourself lately," Darren pressed.

"Yeah," Jimmy replied, sinking further into his seat. "Let's go."

* * *

Jimmy gave a wave before heading into his unlocked house. It was strange for him to just pull the door open. He did so cautiously, regretting not asking his neighbor, Mrs. Austen to watch the house while he was away. Once in, he scanned the hallway to the kitchen, the living room, and the staircase, looking for anything irregular. At first look, nothing seemed out of the ordinary. He strode through the living room, taking in the folded blanket and pillow perfectly placed on the couch, then into the kitchen where he noticed something bizarre; his keys were on the kitchen counter, splayed out as if they were tossed there, haphazardly.

He ripped off his coat in haste to expose his left forearm. The red mark from the belt was gone.

Chapter 11: Jimmy's Soul

Thursday, September 23, 1982 -- 3:01 am

My eyes opened. *I recognize that sound.* I sat up, being careful not to wake Beatrice. I slid out of bed and positioned my glasses over my ears, grabbed my housecoat, then stepped into my slippers and glided toward the bedroom door, looking back at my companion once more before twisting the handle.

Gripping the railing firmly, I carefully descended the stairs, counting each step silently to myself. It was a simple method, but it helped me navigate the stairs without mishap. Arriving in the kitchen, I let out a sigh of relief. It might have seemed silly, but my little routine made dealing with those stairs a bit easier. *Ugh, I really hate these damned stairs!*

Once in the kitchen, I pat the corners of the wall, then the fridge, then Beatrice's chair, and so on. I didn't want to put any lights on, but I struggled to find any living room landmarks without them, so the patting method it was. When finally at the front window, I yanked the drapes apart, revealing the scene outside.

"There! I see him."

In the dim light, I could make out the figure of a man, his shoulders slumped under the weight of a heavy sack, dragging his feet as he trudged along.

I pulled the housecoat tighter around me and took three steps down to the front door, opening it, the fresh cool evening air entered my lungs. It was refreshing. I was anxious to get out there and finally meet one of those people carrying heavy sacks on their backs. I finally saw one in my embodied state.

Once on the driveway, I became discontent with my slowness, grunting in frustration when I finally made it to the curb. All I had to do was make it to that dammed corner of Wellington and Front. The man with the sack was shuffling his feet up Front Street. *Maybe he will answer me this time! Hurry! Move those old bones of yours!*

"Hey!" I called out, but my voice cracked with a mixture of fear and desperation. The man didn't even flinch, his attention seemingly fixed on something in the distance. Those shoes, heavy and worn, scraped against the pavement with each step, the sound echoing off the tall buildings at the four corners, creating an eerie atmosphere.

I could feel tightness in my chest as I struggled to move. When I tried to call again, the discomfort increased to the point I collapsed onto the dry pavement, my knees taking the final blow. Facing the pavement and holding my chest, it took a minute to focus enough to find my glasses, which, when I did, displayed a strand of mucus that ran from my mouth onto them when I fell. I fumbled to put them on, and when I did, the man with the sack was gone.

"Walter," came a call, but it wasn't Beatrice. It was the voice of another woman, with a distinct accent. "Walter Murphy. What are you doing out at this time of night?"

A short, plump, middle-aged woman wearing an overcoat waddled over to me, her steps hurried yet steady. She took my forearm in her hand, her touch warm and reassuring.

"Are you all right?" Her voice had a singing quality to it.

She steadied me, allowing my old body to finally get to my feet, which I struggled with on my own. Once I was upright, I turned to where I had seen the man with the sack and pointed, my hand trembling slightly with the lingering shock.

"Did you see him? That man?"

"Good Lord," the Scottish woman blurted out, her eyes widening with surprise. "You're shiverin'. And you're so pale. Are you sure you're all right? Here, love." She took my arm to guide me to the house. "Let me take you home."

"I can manage," I insisted weakly.

The woman had white curly hair that was so thin you could freely see her pink scalp. She had a pudgy nose, large blue eyes, and thin pink lips on an excessively wrinkled white face for a woman barely fifty. The poor woman must have concluded that I was suffering from dementia, but I truly had no idea who she was. The blank face I made surely confirmed it.

"Walter! You don't know who I am, do you? It's Betty. Your neighbor . . . next door."

I didn't respond. I was truly miserable. I was cold and incredibly uncomfortable from the fall. I wanted nothing more than to just crawl into bed beside Beatrice. I behaved like a child and any social grace I should have displayed towards the kind neighbor went out the window. I wanted to cry.

"Let go of me!" I yelped, feeling the woman's grip tightening.

"Beatrice," the neighbor called urgently from the front door, her voice echoing through the hallway. "Walter's not well."

"Why did you go and wake her up for?" I muttered under my breath. "Now look what you've done."

No matter how serious I wanted that last phrase to sound, it came off sounding like the ramblings of a crazed old man.

"Jimmy," Beatrice's voice carried down the stairs.

"There's no Jimmy, Mrs. Murphy. It's your husband, Walter. He was in the middle of the street."

As I shuffled past the neighbor, she reached out a hand in a gesture of support, her touch grounding me in the moment.

"Oh, my love, please be careful," Betty, the Scottish neighbor, urged.

"What's going on?" Beatrice's voice trembled with a mixture of alarm and bewilderment, her eyes darting between the voices of me and the neighbor's.

"It's Walter. I found him in the middle of the street. He's banged his knees," the neighbor explained gently yet firmly. "Take a seat, Walter. I'll tend to those."

"Can you get me an Aspirin too, please?" I did as the woman asked and plopped myself on my chair. Exhaustion weighed heavily on me, leaving me too drained to do anything else.

Beatrice eased herself into her seat with the neighbor's assistance. "Would someone please tell me what's going on?"

4:30 am
It was a humbling experience, accepting the fact that, no matter what I wanted to achieve, my elderly body couldn't comply. It resulted in me appearing feeble and

confused, angering me in the process. Betty MacFarland was a pleasant woman who made sure the two of us were looked after before she left. I wasn't kind to her while she tended to us. I regretted not showing enough gratitude but I was not in a good state. My body had reminded me of it.

Once the two of us were alone, I reluctantly explained in detail what I had witnessed.

"Are you sure you weren't dreaming?" Beatrice asked, her voice gentle but firm. "You must have been sleepwalking."

"I saw the man. I already told you!" I insisted, my frustration mounting. I wanted to pound my fist on the arm of the chair but managed to restrain myself.

"Oh . . ." She raised her hand slightly as if to wave dismissively, as she usually did, but stopped herself.

I was too perturbed to face her, my mind racing with the vivid image of the man with the sack. We sat in an uneasy silence for a moment, the tension thick between us, before she finally spoke.

"Can I tell you something?" she asked softly, breaking the quiet.

"I suppose so."

"I've had that dream."

"It wasn't a dream, Bea."

"Just listen." She blurted sharply. "And then, you tell me if this sounds familiar."

I nodded.

"During my . . . infidelity, I had a reoccurring dream."

"Go on."

"I remembered . . ." She lifted her head slightly, recollecting her dream. ". . . while still in my nightgown, leaving my bedroom, leaving my house. I was enticed. Perhaps . . . maybe it was more a pull. Before I knew it. I was no longer just . . . walking normally. My steps . . . were heavy. Oh, I strained to bring what was needed. Yes, I needed to bring with me what was on my back . . . and my God, it was heavy. I felt it ache while in that dream. But . . .he needed it."

"Needed what?" I interjected. "Who was . . . he?"

"I don't know for certain." Her bottom lip hung open for a moment, then she finished her thought. "But I think I know."

Frustrated with her delay, I demanded: "Who?"

She hesitated once more before continuing.

"That was the first dream. It was just that. The pull. The heavy load I carried. And then I woke."

"And then...?"

"It continued," she said quietly.

"Tell me!" My voice rose, the anticipation and frustration making me impatient.

"Stop pressuring me! It's difficult to talk about." She exhaled deeply, looking away. "The affair...the affair continued. I told myself...that was it!" She made a cutting motion with both hands horizontally, the gesture sharp and definitive. "I told Arnold it was over, and..."

"Arnold?"

"My lover. The one I had..."

"I see," I responded, feeling a sting as if it were me she had cheated on. I shifted awkwardly in my chair.

"But it didn't end. The love affair continued. I made little attempt to stop it. But..." she cleared her throat, "that dream didn't stop either. I had it again."

"And?"

"It continued where it left off; me, carrying that heavy sack. The first dream seemed endless; it felt like I was destined to move my feet with that heavy load forever. That..." she raised her finger. "That was a weird dream. But the second one...that one was frightening."

I waited for her to continue.

"I had finally arrived. Yes, I knew I was there, and there were others too. I saw them, but I didn't pay attention to who they were. They weren't important. What *was* important was finally delivering what I had been instructed to carry."

"What? What was it?" I asked, leaning forward.

"Coal."

"For what?"

She sat silent for a moment. I studied her face and became extremely uncomfortable with her disposition. Her hands began to shake. Her lips tightened. Whatever dream she had, whatever image imprinted in her mind must have been hauntingly vivid.

She finally faced me.

"Jimmy. I know you have been through a lot. Maybe you have... I don't know... certain abilities. But if you ever hear that..." Beatrice started, her voice trembling. She pulled a tissue out of her housecoat to dab her eyes, her hands shaking. "...that dragging of those shoes. Don't go. Don't go after it again. It's not good."

I leaned in closer. "What happened, Bea?"

She hesitated, her eyes darting around the room as if the shadows themselves held her secrets. "I was feeding it."

"Feeding what?" I demanded.

"I don't want to talk about it. It's too upsetting." She slammed her hands on her chair, the sound sharp and startling. "Let's go to bed."

Saturday, September 25, 1982 -- 3:00 pm

As our guests entered, Beatrice sat at the dining room table with the cakes that we bought from the local bakery. It took much effort but I welcomed the ladies in, taking their coats and umbrellas.

"Bloody rain," Agnes grumbled, her voice dripping with irritation. "It's ruined my perm."

"Oh, stop your complaining," Dolores snapped, rolling her eyes. "Hello, Bea, dear. How are you feeling?"

"Fine, just fine," Beatrice replied, a soft smile on her lips. "My new Walter has been such a sweetheart. Haven't you?"

"I do my best," I said, trying to keep my tone light.

Agnes scrunched her face at my reply, clearly unimpressed. However, her tiny friend was more pleasant. "Hello, Jimmy," Dolores said warmly, then leaned in to kiss her blind friend on the cheek. "You know, I think it's sweet that you have this new friend. I think fate has worked in your favor."

Beatrice's smile grew a little wider, and she reached out to pat my hand.

I sauntered to the kitchen to stand the umbrellas against the wall when I heard Beatrice whisper to her guests, "He likes to cuddle," followed by giggles.

Yes, it was true. I enjoyed having her beside me at night. After spending so much time as a bodiless spirit, and feeling incredibly unwanted, I craved the warmth of a human body. But it wasn't just the physical warmth; it was the closeness of her that truly warmed my soul. It wasn't about intimacy; it was something beautiful. I had no idea how much I needed companionship until then.

"Bring the tea, dear. The girls and I are ready."

I placed the pot and four cups on the platter and paced carefully to the dining room which was in front of the bay window. My hands were shaky, worried about breaking the fancy cups that Beatrice had asked me to put out. I had no idea how difficult it was going to be to balance a pot of hot water and four China cups on a silver platter as an eighty-one-year-old man. Once finally set down, I took the pot in my hand to begin pouring when I was interrupted.

"Let me do that," Dolores chirped squinting her tiny brown eyes, pursing her lips as she took the pot from me. One would think she was being critical, but I read her differently. She glanced at me before taking the teapot from me. It was the first time her eyes met mine. They were inquisitive. It was almost like she was reading me on Bea's behalf. Strange.

"Jimmy," Bea snapped, "stop hovering and take a seat." She gestured to the other end of the table.

"There you go, hon." Dolores placed a cup in front of Beatrice, gently guiding her hand to the handle. Beatrice nodded in appreciation.

"You mentioned this... Host Road," Agnes said, glancing at me. "I don't think there's a Host Road west of town, do you, Lola?" she added, doubtfully, before taking a bite of her carrot cake.

Dolores sat silent for a moment, thinking, her tiny hand holding her child-sized head. Then she raised a finger before saying, "There was a farmer by the name of Llewellyn Host. He must have died at least ten years ago. He was a miserable man by all accounts. But I don't recall a road being named after him."

"I can show you where it is," I chimed in.

The two guests exchanged silent glances, their eyes briefly flitting to Beatrice before returning to me.

"Don't be silly," Beatrice waved off my offer. "You lost your license last year. Well... Walter did. It's still his body."

She reached her arm over to pat the table, leaving it there for me to cover with mine. Agnes's eyes widened in surprise as I complied.

"I'll drive you there," Dolores offered, her eyes flicking between our hands and Beatrice's sunglasses. "That is... unless you two change your minds between now and then." She took a sip from her cup, her gaze still darting back and forth.

"Then it's settled," Beatrice affirmed, positioning her hand by her cup and seeming to fix her gaze on Dolores across the table.

"I don't understand," Agnes blurted out. "What exactly are we going to do?"

"We're going to go to this... this mysterious house and see what... or if... poor Jimmy here can return to his original self," Beatrice explained, her voice tinged with determination.

"But what about the other chap? His original... you know... body? It won't just happen to be there," Agnes interjected.

Beatrice scrunched her face in frustration, evident in her tightened jaw.

"One thing at a time, Ag. Stop being such a Negative Nelly!" She waved her hand in the direction of her friend, knocking some of the pastries off the plate. "I want to see if this house has powers. I need to know what spirits exist there. We'll treat it as a sort of reconnaissance mission," she then leaned toward me. "Walter always appreciated it when I used military terms, although he never fought in any of the wars," Beatrice reminisced.

"Why was that?" I asked.

"You..." she patted my hand gently. "He was ill when he enlisted in the first. Then, well... he wasn't young enough to join the second. It's something we avoided talking about. I know he always felt ashamed that he wasn't able to help liberate Europe. It bothered him immensely." Something swirled in her mind. "Llewellyn Host. That name rings a bell," she mused, her eyes lighting up with determination. Suddenly, she released my hand and slapped it on the dining room table hard. "Let's go tomorrow. I need to know where this... this mysterious place is," Beatrice declared.

"Fine," Dolores said with a resigned sigh, taking a sip from her cup. "I'll give my car a start tomorrow morning to make sure it turns over. I haven't used it in weeks. Besides, it's supposed to be a lovely day Sunday."

Chapter 12: Jimmy's Body and Billy Gibson's Soul

Sunday, September 26, 1982 -- 2:00 pm

Jimmy had been in a funk all weekend. Something was eating at him and it wouldn't stop. He thought to himself, *maybe that pile of horse dung was right. Maybe I need to reunite with my soul.*

"No. That wasn't even real. That was just a bad trip," he muttered to himself. He paused, as if contemplating the validity of his own words. "Or was it?"

With a determined resolve, he hastily changed into his cycling gear, his movements brisk and purposeful. "I need to find out for myself, without any coke this time."

Off he went on his bike, rolling through town and then onto River Road. The familiar route seemed to pass by in a blur as he navigated the winding road, his mind focused on the destination ahead. Finally, he came to a stop on the pavement where he had found his car the week prior.

Placing his left foot on the ground, he studied the house on the hill. It still stood there, imposing yet seemingly ordinary, with a blue Pontiac parked in the gravel driveway. He shook his head, trying to shake off the unsettling feeling that lingered within him.

Still feeling the fright of that evening, he dared not approach the house. Instead, he pushed off and traveled to the entrance of gHost Road, stopping at the pile of horse excrement, twisting his head east and west ensuring he was alone before leaning down.

"Hello!" he called out to the dried-up pile. It was still intact with no tire tracks through it.

Peering up at the winding dirt pathways of gHost Road, he said to himself, "This is so surreal. I don't understand. I suppose it was a bad trip? Or maybe it was a dream?" he mused aloud.

After his short cycle along the bumpy path, stopping at the farmhouse, he rubbed his arms, recollecting the image of the hordes of maggots that poured out from under its frame. He dropped his bike, approached the door then took in a large breath and opened it, looking down at the bottom, making certain that nothing seeped from under it. He exhaled.

Once in, he was drawn to the commanding staircase which he recollected. "Exactly as I remembered. Exactly!" He viewed the living room, peering up at the fallen plaster and the remains of it scattered on the floor below. He peaked into the kitchen before being drawn to the staircase, placing his hand on the newel post, before taking each step slowly, coughing from the dust that stirred as he moved upwards. Near the top, he stopped and swallowed the excess saliva that was collected. With eyes closed, to avoid the onset of dizziness and nausea, he eventually re-opened them. To his relief, the stairs and the top level were still, so he continued until atop.

"Phew!" He took a step forward but stopped at the discovery of the hole in the middle of the hallway. He wasn't immediately drawn by the window across the way. Instead, his focus was elsewhere. He stepped around the large gap and moved down the hall, slowly and mechanically until he reached the room at the end—the bathroom. He placed his hand over his chest in a fruitless attempt to stop his heart from pounding through his ribs. The east-facing window let in enough light to illuminate the tiny bathroom which contained a filthy bathtub. The tub was positioned exactly as he remembered it, except that there was no flesh-less body. Instead, there was a dark brown residue splattered on its yellow enamel. Its stench caused him to cover his mouth and exit the room in haste. Once at the top of the stairs, he turned to where the bedroom was. *That's right. The ghostly image!*

He approached the well-lit bedroom window, peering down at the lush grass when, from the side of the house, an elderly woman with blue-tinted hair emerged.

"Who is that?"

BANG! BANG! BANG! The loud thuds echoed from the main floor, causing him to jerk his head in that direction.

"Someone's here!" he exclaimed.

From the other side of the door below, a tiny voice called out.

Focused on the staircase, he sprinted toward the landing when, moments later, he found himself sprawled on the living room floor. Chunks of plaster fell onto his face as he lay there, staring up at the ceiling.

* * *

As he gradually regained consciousness, a wave of pain rushed through him, leaving him barely able to move.

"Agh!" he gasped, his face contorting in agony.

Struggling to lift his head, he glanced down to see his left foot twisted at an odd angle. The realization hit him like a ton of bricks – it was broken. Even the slightest movement of his left arm sent sharp, shooting pains through his body. He lay on his back, shutting his eyes tightly to shield them from the particles of dust swirling around him.

"Hello," he croaked, his voice barely audible above the throbbing in his head. After a few moments, he mustered all his strength to utter a faint plea. "Help!"

7:45 pm

As the dim afternoon glow faded into darkness through the western windows, Jimmy kept his eyes closed, the shivering finally subsiding. Then, he felt it – a profound shift in his being.

It was as if a heavy weight had been lifted from his chest, a release he could sense deep within him. The presence that had once occupied his body, the entity known as Billy Gibson, was gone.

Now it was just the physicality of him once again. He felt broken and feeble and abandoned, just like the house he occupied. The pain of his broken-down body mercifully subsided. The grip of its agony gave way, finally allowing it to remain still and at peace; a process in which signals sent were unanswered, much like a broken radio circuit. The pings continued, but when ignored, they ceased and thus did his heartbeat.

Chapter 13: Jimmy's Soul

Sunday, September 26, 1982 -- 2:30 pm

"Ready?" I asked tentatively, my hand hovering near Beatrice's arm. "First step..."

"Oh, nonsense! I've done this a million times. Just take my hand as I go. You're a dear and all, but I'm not an invalid."

"Yes, Bea."

Agnes, her newly permed hair sporting a fresh tint of blue, stood beside the car, the rear door already open for us. Once we descended the steps, I continued holding Beatrice's free hand until we reached the car, letting her move into the back seat before me.

"You are a true gentleman," Agnes said, offering a rare compliment, her tone warm with genuine appreciation. It was the first positive sign she had given me since I took over Walter's body. I settled in beside Beatrice as Agnes shut the door and climbed into the passenger seat.

"All ready, you two?" Dolores asked, peering at us through the rearview mirror.

"All set."

The memory of my bike ride came flooding in while Dolores drove onto River Road, the car chugging up it slowly. She was a very cautious and capable driver, which I appreciated. I sat up as we approached the field of Holsteins and then the backdrop of the tall maples. I pointed before I could speak, passing gHost Road.

"There," I said, craning my neck to the far right as we passed it.

"Oh, for heaven's sake. I don't see anything," Dolores grumbled.

Our bodies shifted forward as our driver brought the car to an abrupt stop.

"Where did you say it was?" Dolores asked, putting the car in park.

I twisted to peer out the rear window. "There. See the house at the end of the road?"

Dolores got out of the car, holding her purse close to her. Still seated, I followed her movements and rolled down the window. Agnes followed her friend who took a step on the dirt road and peered up at the graffiti-laden sign.

"Well, it's a true road all right," Delores remarked, her tone tinged with skepticism as she surveyed the surroundings.

"Come on, Ag," she urged, gesturing for her friend to follow. Then, addressing us, she added, "You two stay here."

I watched intently as Beatrice and Agnes cautiously navigated through the tire paths, their footsteps leaving imprints in the soft earth. The two disappeared from view, swallowed by the eerie ambiance of the secluded road. After what felt like an eternity, I turned to Beatrice, noticing the tightness of her lips.

"What is it?" I asked.

"Shush!" she responded sharply, her eyes darting around warily.

I studied her tense face. I knew from experience not to prompt her, but to wait and let her describe what she was experiencing. It didn't take her long.

"I don't like it," Beatrice muttered, her voice tight with apprehension.

"What? What is it?"

"I sense something very bad is about to happen." She turned to me, urgency flickering in her gaze. "Call them."

Without hesitation, I reached for the door handle and pushed the car door open.

"Dolores!" I called out.

In the distance, I could hear Dolores banging and calling at the door of the mysterious house.

"Dolores! Agnes! Don't go in. Come back, please," I pleaded, waving frantically to catch their attention.

"All right, all right, we're coming," Dolores's tiny voice replied from afar.

I stepped onto the dirt road but stopped. The intrigue I felt weeks ago had transposed into an anxiety I hadn't anticipated. I felt fearful for the two women but was relieved when I saw the blue hair bobbing in my direction from the distance. I waited, hunched over, wondering how long my decrepit body would hold me up without support.

"Are they coming?" Beatrice called from the car.

"Yes. I see them. They're fine."

"Thank God."

Waiting at the end of the road, wobbling like a balloon on a string, I remained stationary until they arrived.

"Jimmy, for heaven's sake! What are you doing out of the car?" Agnes exclaimed, her grip firm as she took me by the arm. "Come on, let's get you in."

"What did you see?" I asked.

"Later," Dolores chimed in. "There's something very disturbing about that place."

"I felt it," Beatrice added, her tone grave and solemn.

Once in the car, Dolores made a poorly executed three-point turn, running over the pile of horse dung, before speeding along River Road.

* * *

The three of us gathered around the living room as Agnes boiled the kettle in the kitchen.

"Tell us, Dolores," Agnes called out. "What happened? What did you see?"

Dolores took a deep breath, her hands clasped tightly in her lap. She glanced around the room, as if gathering her thoughts, before speaking. "Well..." she began, her voice wavering slightly. "The house... It wasn't abandoned."

"What do you mean? I've been there," I interjected.

Dolores hesitated. "There was someone inside. I heard movement," she continued, her tone growing more solemn.

"That couldn't be..." I protested.

Agnes, who had been bustling in the kitchen, paused to listen. "There was a bike sitting in the driveway," she chimed in, her voice carrying into the room.

"That's mine."

"Well, that's probably where you left it when you separated from your body," she snapped.

"That doesn't make sense. Jimmy took it home that day. And then . . . the other day, when I followed him, he drove it . . ." I stopped as a horrible thought had come over me.

As the tense atmosphere thickened, Beatrice, who had remained silent until then, finally spoke up. "An evil spirit resides in that place."

"I think he's in trouble," I said. I attempted to stand, but Walter's stiff joints refused to cooperate, keeping me firmly rooted to the spot.

9:30 pm

As I tried to put my mind to rest as to Jimmy's whereabouts, Beatrice and I began our routine readying ourselves for bed. Oh yes. The routine. It was strangely natural and something I secretly looked forward to. There were several reasons. I found that my posture became worse as the day carried on. Before I knew it, I was hunched over to avoid the pain of straightening up. Lying in bed at the end of the day was my relief. But there was that twenty minutes or so when I lay flat, waiting for the signal. It never failed. I glowed in anticipation of it.

"Jimmy," Bea said softly, reaching out her right hand as she remained lying on her left side. "Come."

As usual, I scooted over and pressed my body against hers, enjoying the lovely radiance. I don't think I could ever fully describe it because it garnered so many feelings and sensations. But it started with human warmth. Not just a humanly body's warmth, but *hers* specifically; it was an adoration for someone I cared for, someone who cared for me. Age didn't play a part anymore. Although I was no longer a thirty-one-year-old man, I still enjoyed the pleasures of human functions, the blood that flowed, providing the joy of touch and warmth. The evening snuggles were magical, and if I died that night while cuddling, I would be content. But anxiety got the better of me. It wasn't Jimmy's whereabouts that concerned me. It was the worry that Beatrice may not be there when I woke.

As she broke from our embrace and lay flat, I became confused because of her sudden change. "Jimmy," she said softly, her voice wavering.

"Yes, Bea?"

"I don't think I said this outright, but... in case you weren't sure, I'd be just as happy if you would stay in Walter's body. I just assumed that you wanted your original back."

I was taken aback by her admission, unsure of how to respond. I remained silent, contemplating her words, while her sightless eyes seemed to search for something unseen.

"I hadn't made that decision yet," I finally admitted.

She turned towards me, taking my hand and placing it across her chest. She said something but her words were barely audible.

"Sorry, Bea. I didn't hear you," I said softly, leaning closer to catch her words.

"It's nothing," she replied, her grip tightening on my hand as she sniffled softly.

I wrapped my arms around her, pulling myself against her tiny frame.

That was the moment I fell in love with Beatrice Murphy. It was the first time I had ever fallen in love.

Tuesday, September 28, 1982 -- 7:00 am
It was that morning when I could fully appreciate the saying "Count your blessings." Every morning since then,

I woke with the hopes that I could spend another day with Beatrice and her wonderful soul.

Witnessing how Walter's soul had left her without notice, I realized that either of us could go at any moment, day or night. It wasn't fear, it was respect, an appreciation for how precious time had become to me in my new form. I accepted it wholeheartedly.

I was happy to hear the clanking noises she made when filling up the kettle in the kitchen. It was my morning wake-up call which I looked forward to.

2:30 pm
"What the dickens is taking those two so long?" Bea exclaimed as she tapped her foot impatiently. "They should have been here hours ago!"

Beatrice was understanding of the fact that I was concerned for my former body, and so her friends promised to take a discreet stroll by my house that day to snoop around for my green Saab. I determined that if it was still in the driveway by midday then there was cause for concern. They were to return with an update. I tried to occupy my mind by completing the crossword puzzle from the morning's paper, but I was constantly distracted by either the noises my stomach made or the sound of the chickadees outside the window. The little bird's chirps and whistles were a welcome diversion, but even that was broken by something incredibly disturbing: the sound of a siren. Its piercing horn echoed off the buildings of the four corners of town.

"Oh dear," she cried. "I hope they're all right." She motioned to me with her finger. "Jimmy, pick up the phone and dial Dolores for me, will you?"

"OK," I responded, laying the newspaper on the side table. I shuffled across the room to fetch her personal phone book when I heard the doorbell ring.

"I pray to God that's them," Beatrice said, straightening herself in her chair.

My knees had been sore, but I managed to get down a few steps and take a deep breath before opening the large wooden door.

"There you are!" I exclaimed with relief.

"Finally!" Beatrice uttered.

I didn't expect to be able to read Agnes's face, as she never held any emotion; however, Dolores's expression was unmistakably worried. The slight tremble in her hands spoke volumes.

"What happened?" I demanded urgently. "What did you find out? Was the Saab still in the driveway?"

"It's not good," Agnes blurted out, her voice slightly shaky, as Dolores rushed to take off her jacket.

"Let me sit down first," Dolores said, her movements hurried yet deliberate, handing me her jacket. I waited for Agnes to remove her sweater, grunting slightly as I reached up to hang them on the bar in the closet.

"Well, girls. What's the verdict?" Beatrice asked, her tone filled with apprehension and anticipation.

Dolores clasped her hands between her knees, waiting for me to take my seat. She didn't raise her head when she spoke.

"Well . . . we took a walk by, alright. Yes, the green Saab was there and . . . and so was a police car. Agnes, here, knows the neighbor, Glenda Austen, so she moseyed on over and..."

"Yes," I affirmed, nodding in agreement.

Dolores finally raised her head. "The young man was found dead at the farmhouse we visited. The police determined that he fell through to the first floor from the second."

"Oh, no!" Beatrice gasped, bringing her hand to her mouth in shock.

I remained motionless.

"Apparently, it was his boss that contacted the police. He hadn't shown up to work since the Friday before. Glenda said that they believed he had been in that house for a few days. Poor man. I can't believe his family didn't even . . ." Dolores paused, her expression turning somber as she glanced at me. "I'm sorry. I keep forgetting."

What Dolores had communicated was correct, I had torched every relationship with my family. The damage I had done wasn't just between me and Jimmy, it was with all members of my family. I was too embarrassed to admit that I hadn't thought about my mother or my two brothers for months. 'Don't expect me around this Christmas,' was the last thing I said to Mother. We had a disagreement and I blurted that before storming out of the house.

"Jimmy?"

"Yes, Bea?"

"Are you all right?"

I couldn't look up. I hung my head, feeling the weight of emotion pressing down on me. I then covered my watery eyes, trying to hide the turmoil within.

Monday, October 4, 1982 -- 11:00 am
Fall had arrived as the air was cold and the leaves had turned. There was a bitter wind that ran through my frail body, and the dampness from the previous day's rain inflamed my joints. The four of us stood close together, but far enough away from the handful of people who attended the burial of Jimmy. Those in attendance were my brothers, Sid and Frank, my mother, and a few others whom I couldn't make out from the distance. With their backs facing us, I wasn't able to determine their expressions. I was curious and anxious.

There was something else that came over me while I stood in the cemetery; it was the fact that the real Jimmy Sandringham wasn't in the ground. Jimmy's body was, but he wasn't really anything without me. I suppose part of him was: his flesh, his blood, and his nervous system. Although my body ached more since I'd been housed in a much older one, I still held the same feelings of touch, fear, and so many other emotions. But still, it was uncanny watching those who gathered to pay their respects doing so to a broken down and soon-to-be decomposed body. I was still present, within feet of them. What was strange to me was how they would all bid farewell to the grave and move on from it as if my soul was buried with it – bizarre. Perhaps I was fortunate enough to witness my funeral under the camouflage of another. *Do other bodiless souls get to do this?*

"Excuse me," a woman of about forty, with blonde hair and glasses approached us after the guests started to break away from the mound of dirt. I recognized her as Karen, my brother Sid's girlfriend. "The family is going to be gathering at the hall behind the church. There'll be tea and coffee and sandwiches."

I was about to decline but was cut off.

"Of course," Beatrice replied. "We'd be honored."

Karen waved politely and returned with the group of mourners.

"I'm not sure if that's a good idea," I said.

"Nonsense! I'm not going to let you go home and wonder what took place at your own funeral reception."

"Maybe he's right, Bea," Agnes interjected.

My companion waved her hand at her old friend and tugged my coat sleeve, "Come on."

* * *

The four of us were the first to take our seats at a large round table. Although I wasn't hungry, the others started picking at their sandwiches: salmon, tuna, egg salad, and chicken salad, all cut into neat triangles without crusts. I watched them, feeling uneasy and out of place. The light chatter and polite laughter seemed odd given the circumstances. Beatrice, sitting beside me, smiled now and then, trying to be comforting, but even her warmth couldn't chase away the chill inside me.

I was about to take another sip of my coffee when I noticed Karen scoot beside Dolores, who angled her ear to listen better. As Dolores spoke, I kept an eye on Karen, expecting her to look up at me. She didn't. Instead, she nodded, fully engaged in whatever Dolores was saying. Their exchange didn't last long. Karen pulled out her notepad and pen, jotted something down, thanked Dolores, and returned to her table beside my brothers who were enjoying the church-made sandwiches.

Friday, October 8, 1982 -- 10:00 pm

"I still don't like this idea, Bea," I exclaimed, plopping myself onto my chair. Dolores made a sideways glance at her friend, while Agnes raised her eyebrows in agreement.

Beatrice just waved at me, not even bothering to open her mouth. I supposed that was expected after I brought it up three times in the last hour.

It all started the afternoon Karen approached Dolores at the funeral reception and asked her how we knew of "Jimmy." Dolores was quick on her toes and explained that she met his spirit during one of their communications with the other side. The three women decided, without my consent, to host another séance and invite Karen. I didn't care for the premeditated nature of the invitation, but it would give me – well, "my spirit" – the ability to express my sorrows to my family.

I stood quickly upon hearing the knock at the door. "I'll get it," I said, the smooth soles of my slippers allowing me to cross the living room with ease.

"Don't be a fool," Beatrice waved. "You'll give the whole thing away."

From the corner of my eye, I noticed her following the sound of my slippers dragging toward the door as I disobeyed her command. Her fingers clenched the armrest and her lips pressed into a thin line. I took a deep breath, trying to steady my nerves, and opened the door. "Hello, Karen. I'm Walter. Please, come in," I greeted, trying to sound natural. My voice came out a bit too high, but I hoped she didn't notice.

"Nice to meet you," Karen replied, stepping inside. The chill from outside followed her in.

The rain droplets rolled off her coat as she leaned over to remove her boots. I peeked out the open door to witness the steady stream of rain splashing into the puddles outside. I had to be careful not to seem too pleased to see her. I even surprised myself with how excited I was to be in the company of a relative after so long. Karen was always a vibrant woman. I missed her pleasant smile, although that evening, she displayed a nervous one.

"Come in, come in," I said following her up into the living Room. "You remember Dolores," I said.

"For God's sake, Walter, of course she remembers," Beatrice's voice sounded impatient, a sharp contrast to the hushed tones of the room. She stood presenting her hand in mid-air for a moment. Karen rushed to greet her. Meanwhile, I sank into my chair, feeling a little embarrassed by how Bea snapped at me.

"Thank you for coming," Beatrice finally acknowledged Karen.

"Thank you for having me," Karen replied, her voice trembling slightly. "I'm honored you ladies..." She trailed off, still holding Bea's hand firmly, then turned to me, "and gentleman . . . would have me over for one of your meetings with the spirits."

"Please, have a seat," Beatrice gestured towards the couch, her movements slow and deliberate.

"It's so late," Karen remarked with an awkward grin, her eyes darting nervously around the room. "I feel as if I'm intruding."

"Oh, goodness," Beatrice waved her hand dismissively. "We nap for most of the afternoon before one of these things."

Karen shifted in her seat, her unease evident in the way she fidgeted with her watch.

"Bea has the ability," Dolores interjected, her voice causing Karen to jump in her chair. "She's the one they reach out to."

"The spirits?"

"Yes," Dolores confirmed, her gaze fixed on Karen.

Beatrice rocked her head ever so slightly, accepting the compliment from her friend. She was in her glory as she stared across the room as if ignoring our new guest temporarily before turning to face her once again.

"Tell me... what is your reason for coming? Is it to connect with his spirit? Is there something you were hoping to hear, or maybe tell him?"

Karen clenched her hands together, her fingers twisting nervously as she avoided making eye contact. Her gaze fell to the orange shag carpet beneath her feet, and she took a deep breath before speaking.

"I suppose..." She paused, as if uncertain of her own thoughts. Slowly, she raised her head to meet the eyes of the three women before her. "I guess I don't really know." Her voice shook slightly. I leaned in, hanging on her every word as she struggled to find the right ones.

"It happened so suddenly," she began, her voice trembling. "We didn't get a chance to say goodbye. I suppose we wanted to let him know..." She trailed off, her voice catching in her throat. "That he was loved," she continued. "I wanted to tell him that... that he was loved, unconditionally."

She shook her head. "None of us are perfect," she continued. "His brothers miss him, and his mother... well, she's simply heartbroken."

Agnes sat upright suddenly as I wiped a tear that I couldn't contain.

"J..." Beatrice began, then corrected herself, "Walter?" Her voice faltered as she noticed my sniffles. I quickly tried to compose myself.

"Oh, he's sentimental that way," Agnes interjected, her gaze shifting between me and Beatrice. "You know how he is, Bea."

I nodded, grateful for Agnes's attempt to deflect attention away from my moment of vulnerability. Feeling the need to gather myself, I hurried to the kitchen and grabbed a tea towel to blot my eyes, hoping to conceal my emotions.

"Let's get you some tea, Walter," Agnes said, following me into the kitchen and placing the kettle on the stove. "Karen, won't you have some tea as well?"

"That would be lovely."

Saturday, October 9, 1982 -- 12:04 am

"Walter isn't going to join us," Beatrice said as I took my seat away from the card table.

Karen sat where I normally would, her back facing me. We had pre-arranged what my companion would say when the time arrived. I crossed my arms as I sat. I was still perturbed by the disingenuous act, but I can't say I was completely innocent on the matter either.

With the exception of Dolores, the three women rested their fingertips on the planchette. Dolores sat with notepad and pen in hand, the room glowing orange by the four candles Agnes lit earlier. The flicker of the flame at the card table created a jittery shadow of Agnes's poofy hair against the wall, causing me to smirk as it prompted the comparison to an oversized brain.

Beatrice tilted her head upwards, reminiscent of the first evening I met her. She was focused even though I couldn't see her eyes. Being accustomed to her body language, I found her easier to read the more time I spent with her.

"Close your eyes, everyone," Dolores instructed. I followed suit, letting the darkness behind my eyelids envelop me.

"Speak to us, oh kind spirit. This is Beatrice," her voice echoed softly, her head tilted upward in a reverent posture. "Speak to me, kind spirit."

The silence was disturbed by the wheezing of Agnes's exhales; I found its rhythm unsettling. I was finally relieved of it by the soft hiss of the planchette's movement. I decided to open my eyes and study Dolores. She sat perfectly still, her lips pressed tightly together, watching the planchette with impenetrable focus. Her eyes followed its every move with an intensity that seemed almost otherworldly. As the notetaker, her left hand rested lightly on her lap, her right ready to record any message.

The board slid, stopped, then slid then stopped. This noise was interrupted by Beatrice sniffing the air. When the movement of the tiny pointer finally came to a halt, Dolores called out: "It's Walter."

My blind companion remained still. She didn't attempt to speak as the planchette moved several more times. I stood up with the purpose of reading the letters but had to return to my chair and close my eyes when the notetaker glared at me with discontent.

I listened intently to the sliding, dragging sound, holding my breath in anticipation of the eventual outcome.

"He says... he says," Dolores paused, her voice trembling slightly. ". . . I want to come back."

The movement resumed, the sound of sliding and shifting filling the room until finally, Dolores spoke again. "He says... I miss you, my love."

Slowly, I opened my eyes, eager to witness Beatrice's reaction. Her face was illuminated by a wide grin, and I couldn't help but understand the significance of her expression.

Dolores didn't turn to look at me, but I knew she could sense the emotions playing across my face, emotions I couldn't conceal. I felt unwanted again. I was ashamed and embarrassed for having taken on another man's body. As the insecurity of the event grew, I sensed the flush of blood to my face—my hands shook. I was consumed by an unsettling mix of emotions; embarrassment mingled with jealousy, creating a bitter taste in my mouth. It was hard to accept that Beatrice still harbored feelings for Walter, even in his absence. The desire to escape from this situation grew stronger with each passing moment.

My mind raced, searching for a way to extricate myself from this body and the uncomfortable situation it brought. But the thought of facing the unknown consequences of being without a body filled me with dread. I wasn't prepared to confront death in its entirety, not yet.

The planchette hadn't stopped moving. The tiny woman

continued watching it shift and stop, noting each letter producing the final sentence.

"He says . . . I'm ready, Bea." I sat up straighter, my eyes fixed on the women's hands as they hovered over the planchette.

"He says . . ." Dolores paused, making a note before continuing, "Jimmy . . . must leave my body . . . will . . . willingly."

Agnes sucked in a breath loudly and Karen turned to her, "What does that mean?"

"Shhh. Close your eyes, please," Dolores urged.

Walter's message continued to unfold.

"If not . . ." Dolores's voice wavered slightly, "He says . . ." She trailed off, her brow wrinkled in concentration. "He says . . . I'll create one . . . from Arnold."

I stood up abruptly, struggling to process what I had just heard.

The sudden movement caused the planchette to fall from the board, clattering loudly against the floor.

"Goodbye," Dolores called before reaching for the fallen pointer.

Beatrice rose from her seat, her expression grave. "Take me upstairs, please."

While the tiny woman escorted Beatrice, my companion didn't make any acknowledgment of my presence when she passed. She always made a gesture of some sort. Not that night.

I was frightful at the thought of turning to face Agnes and Karen, so I ignored them. Instead, I returned to my seat and studied the pale green carpet.

"Jimmy?" Karen's voice cut through the heavy silence. In the periphery, I could see Agnes, her hand covering her mouth in shock.

I met Karen's gaze and nodded slowly. "Yes, it's me."

She reached out, placing her hand gently on mine. "I'm not sure what's going on, but I think you got mixed up in some sort of witchcraft," she leaned in and whispered. "Which one's the witch?"

I shook my head, feeling a weight of guilt settle in my chest. "No one, Karen. It's all my fault. Well . . . most of it."

"He's a good soul," Agnes interjected, her voice shaky as she pushed herself away from the card table. "This wasn't supposed to happen tonight." With a hurried pace, she made her way toward the stairs, muttering to herself, "This is not good. No, not good at all. Oh, poor Bea."

3:15 am

"I'm sorry," Beatrice murmured, her blind gaze fixed on the ceiling above the bed. "I'm keeping you awake."

I shifted. "It's alright. I can't sleep either."

Although still feeling the sting of being given my eviction notice, I couldn't help but feel sorry for Beatrice. Her husband wanted to return, but he threatened to end the life of her past lover, Arnold Baker, if I didn't leave his body willingly. In an awkward display of affection, she insisted I join her in bed because she didn't know how much time we would have together. This softened the blow I had earlier as I had come to love the woman and was hurt by her insensitive grin.

As for Karen, I had no choice but to divulge my situation. We spent an hour in the basement painfully reliving my story. But I also took the opportunity to tell her of my regrets and how I missed my family. I begged her not to disclose any of my story to my brothers or mother unless I needed to vacate Walter's body and venture to the other side.

"Do you want me to go downstairs so you can sleep?" Beatrice asked softly, her hand reaching out to gently squeeze my forearm.

"No, I don't want you to go. Stay, please," I replied, feeling the warmth of her touch comforting me. I gazed at the outline of her face in the dim light, noticing the way her eyes moved thoughtfully.

"The choice isn't yours, Jimmy. It's mine. I'll take the burden off of you," Beatrice said.

"A man shouldn't die because of this," I protested.

"Shush! You're not going anywhere. Besides..." Beatrice paused, her expression softening.

"What?" I prompted.

"I need you. Arnold doesn't deserve to die, but I've fallen for you."

I didn't respond immediately. There was something else weighing on my mind, something I chose to keep to myself.

Thursday, October 14, 1982 -- 3:00 pm

I had made the decision while sitting in the basement after Beatrice was chaperoned upstairs by Dolores. I'd concocted a plan to visit gHost Road and knew I had a limited window of opportunity to do so. Every Thursday afternoon my blind companion and her friends washed, permed and sometimes colored each other's hair. Dolores would pick Bea up and the three women would have tea and pastries and chat about town gossip. I'm sure I was the topic of recent gatherings. Therefore, unbeknownst to Beatrice, I left the house. It was the best time to make my move.

There I was, standing by the front window, fully dressed with coat and hat, peeking out from the curtain as a child would, spying on a parent. The adolescent feeling quickly fled when the cab pulled into the driveway. I even had my shoes on so as not to keep the cabbie waiting for fear he would honk the horn.

Once I gained the driver's attention, I shuffled to the rear of the car where I struggled to open the heavy door.

"Don't worry, I got it," I replied, my tone dripping with sarcasm.

"Where to?" the driver asked, glancing at me through the rearview mirror.

"Asphodel sixth line," I said, smoothing down my pants with gloved hands, a habit I'd picked up from Beatrice. The driver seemed hesitant at my request, but I needed to get as close to gHost Road as possible without raising suspicion.

"Sixth line?" he repeated, turning his head slightly. "What number?"

"Just drop me off at the corner of Asphodel and River," I said hastily, sensing his reluctance.

"Alright, mister," the driver replied, shifting the car into reverse and backing out of the driveway.

3:10 pm

Although I never doubted her sincerity, I still felt it was time to venture into unknown territory once again. I determined that nothing was going to change for me unless I ventured to that abandoned farmhouse on gHost Road. If something was going to happen, it was to take place where all my problems started. I wasn't looking forward to what may lie ahead, but I had no other choice. I needed out of Walter's body and that was the only place for it to happen.

The exhaust fumes caused me to cough as the cab pulled away, and I watched as it disappeared over the hill before I headed up River Road. It was sunny, which was encouraging, but I did struggle with the amount of effort required to haul my carriage along the paved road. I was almost out of breath when I approached the trees that hid the entrance to gHost Road. I stopped and leaned over, my hands on my knees, and the blood rushing to my head. The short rest was welcoming. After the break, and once passed the foliage, the winding dirt road was finally in view. I stood, gritting my teeth; not because of the final destination, but how I was to maneuver to it. I determined that it was better to walk on the tall grass than on the uneven tire paths. I sighed heavily before pressing on. In that moment, all the feelings flooded back—the hour and seven-minute delay, and the sting of Jimmy's rejection. *Why did it have to be me? What did it all mean?*

Barely halfway to the farmhouse, I needed to stop to catch my breath once again. Whatever dampness and chill I felt in the cab had all but disappeared. I was burning up from the effort and my breathing was strained. I bent over, placing my hands on my knees again, "Maybe this wasn't such a good idea."

I tore my gloves off and threw them aside. I stood and unzipped my jacket, feeling the cool autumn air bless my neck and chest.

Once at the house, I hesitated on the doorstep, soaking in the last rays of the afternoon sun casting its golden light across the sky.

"Perhaps this is the last time I'll see you, my friend," I murmured, a sense of finality weighing on my heart.

Gathering my resolve, I took a deep breath. "I believe I'm ready... for what's next."

As I mustered my courage, the door creaked open, releasing a familiar sour odor that filled my senses. I coughed, the dust swirling around me, a stark reminder of the neglect it had endured. With a steadying breath, I placed my hand on the worn wooden post, my gaze fixed on the daunting staircase ahead. Summoning all my strength, I gripped the railing tightly and took my first tentative step, the old floorboards groaning beneath my weight. "There. That wasn't so bad," I whispered to myself, mustering determination for the journey ahead. "OK. One more. Come on. You can do it!"

I continued this until the fifth step. That's when I was slowed by a thrust of energy. The pressure wasn't just internal; it felt like an external force pushing me down, making each step a struggle.

"I've got to do this," I grunted, my hand gripping the railing tightly for support. Bending over, I fought to catch my breath. It wasn't easy, but I dared not look down, afraid I might lose my footing and fall.

"There's no going back. You've got to keep going," I reminded myself, steeling my resolve despite the growing burden weighing me down. With each step up the staircase, the pressure intensified, even as every fiber of my being screamed to turn back. I even surprised myself with the ability to keep climbing. With three more steps, I fought the push of gravity and labored upwards until at the top, which was when I closed my eyes to avoid the room revolving. That sensation was almost identical to what Jimmy and I had experienced. I was prepared for it. If I hadn't, it would have certainly caused me to fall. I waited for what seemed minutes before I opened my eyes. I released my hand from the top post, and then moved to the bedroom window, so focused on it that I almost landed in the large hole in the hallway. Skirting around it, I forgot how far down it was. The fear of heights seemed to be greater in Walter's body.

Once around, I was able to regain focus on the bedroom window. When I peered out, I was unmoved, as nothing seemed out of the ordinary. This concerned me as I foolishly expected something unusual to happen. However, any further consideration for what was on the other side of the window was disrupted by a hammering sound coming through the house, startling me.

"What was that?" I murmured, stepping cautiously toward the hallway and peering down at the large hole. Everything seemed undisturbed, unchanged. But then, a tapping noise echoed through the house, breaking the silence. Curious, I followed the sound, shuffling over to the radiator where it seemed to originate.

"Did the boiler just kick on?" I wondered aloud, feeling a slight change in temperature. Shivering, I lowered myself to the floor, leaning against the radiator for warmth. The dampness of the house seemed to seep into my bones, leaving me feeling chilled and weary. I closed my eyes briefly to rest, but that plan didn't work out so well.

6:40 pm

I opened my eyes to darkness, momentarily disoriented and unsure of my surroundings. With a feeble voice, I called out, "Beatrice?"

My back was sweaty and began to burn from the heat from the radiator. The house was pitch black, save a glow penetrating from the hole in the hallway floor. The sound of a distant roar and crackle that came from it was alarming. There was something else that I could hear far below; it was the sound of metal scraping on concrete. I'd heard that sound before.

"What *is* that?" I muttered, pulling off my jacket and tossing it aside with my hat. *Is that . . . shoveling? What's happening? It's so uncomfortably hot!*

I squirmed, attempting to stand, but my efforts were futile. "Dammit!"

Regret flooded me as I realized it was a bad decision to sit on the floor. I tried again to stand, but my joints were seized.

"Sitting on the floor, like a ten-year-old. What were you thinking, Ji . . . ?"

The scraping noise persisted.

"Where is that . . . that noise coming from?"

While on my hands and knees, I moved closer to the large opening until at its perimeter. That's when a large chunk of the floor broke free, falling below. I retreated for fear of the floor collapsing, but also from the extreme heat emitting from it. The strange noise continued. I waited a minute before encroaching on the gaping hole once more. Beneath were no longer the scattered remains of plaster on the living room floor, but a large orange glow from a huge fire, flames darting from its hot embers. That's when I saw it, the tip of a shovel tossing coal onto the fire. *Is that what all that coal was for? Those people I saw, they were carrying the sacks on their backs for . . . for this fire.*

"I don't want to die like this. I don't deserve to burn in hell. Was I such a bad person? Am I a bad soul?"

I felt the floor beneath me weaken, so I quickly drew back again, which was a wise decision as another large chunk of the floor gave way, leaving an even greater opening and no way for me to move without risking my life.

I dragged myself back to the wall under the window, then stared out at the shadow of the banister lit up by the fire below. I couldn't escape down the stairs. I couldn't lift myself and I wasn't ready to die. I was brave while in my warm bed the night before, but I wasn't ready to face death. I wasn't ready to leave this world.

"Bea?" I called out. "I'm sorry. I should have stayed home." Tears streamed down my face, mingling with the sweat of fear and desperation. "I'm so alone here. This is not how I want to go." I glanced around at the stark yellowed walls, illuminated by the flickering orange flames below.

"There's no one to hold me," I added weakly, my body shaking with grief. "I don't want to die alone."

All the memories of my past life flooded back, especially my neglect of Jimmy and the way I criticized him.

"I was reckless. I neglected you," I confessed, my voice choked with emotion. "I'm sorry, Jimmy."

I let it all out, every ounce of sorrow and regret pouring from me in a torrent of tears. All I wanted was to stay on earth, to be a good person, to have a second chance at life. I begged for it with every fiber of my being, praying for redemption.

With my head now in my hands and my skin turning red and dry, preparing for the ultimate end, the sound of shoveling suddenly stopped. That's when the door creaked open from below.

I raised my head from my hands and pressed myself tighter against the wall, my heart pounding in my chest. *Who is that?*

Then, the familiar crack of the first step, followed by the second. *Who could that be? Is it . . .*

"Jimmy?" I called out, my voice trembling with hope as I sat upright. "Is that you?"

No. It couldn't be him. He's dead.

The steps grew steadier now, each one punctuated by a creak or a snap.

A shadow emerged, and I confirmed it wasn't Jimmy. The ominous figure projected onto the wall was hunched, with a large beak-like nose atop a small head, all perched atop a long, thin neck.

I sucked in a breath, anticipating the man and his shovel coming after me. My arms and hands were shaking. *This is it. This is how I'm going to go. Oh, God. Please forgive me.*

There was one last step before the figure emerged.

"Hey, pal. You OK?"

I remained seated, my back stuck to the wall, still taking in the familiar voice.

"Fred? Is that . . . is that you?" I managed.

"You're shaking. Come on. Let me help you." Fred leaned over, reaching out to me with a reassuring hand under my arm, lifting me gently.

"Up you go. There!" His grip steadied me, but I still felt unsteady, wobbling as he held on. "You OK?" he asked again.

I hesitated. There was something about Fred's presence, something that drew me to the man's eyes. I wasn't looking at them as I normally would. I wasn't judging him. No. Instead, I relented. I had given in. It was as if I could trust him without question, as if he could see through the walls I had built around myself. Any fight I had that kept the vault doors of my emotions closed became instantaneously unlocked. I don't know what caused me to surrender so effortlessly, but I did. In that moment, I let go of my defenses. It was a surrender unlike any I had experienced before, and with it came a sense of liberation—I was free.

* * *

Time seemed to whisk by, the passage marked by the gradual cooling of my body and the easing of my discomfort. My knees, which had been achy, now felt strangely light.

Fred gently tugged at my arm. "Come on. Let's get you downstairs," he urged, but I hesitated, my gaze fixated on the ominous opening in the floor.

"The hole," I murmured nervously, gesturing towards it.

"Don't worry. I'll guide you. Just hold onto my arm," Fred reassured me, his voice a beacon of stability.

I nodded, my nerves still jittery with apprehension.

"Ready?" Fred inquired, and as we moved through the room, I couldn't tear my eyes away from the gaping void below.

"The fire. It's gone out," I observed, my voice tinged with disbelief. Only the remnants of charred plaster remained.

"Don't look down. Just follow me, OK?" Fred instructed.

I nodded again, my grip tightening on his arm as we approached the top of the stairs.

"Now," he continued, "I'm going ahead of you. You just hold onto my arm with your left and grab onto the rail with your other," he directed, patting the solid wood. "Ready? One at a time, OK?"

With each careful step, Fred counted, his pace deliberate and measured.

"I'm shaking," I confessed, the tremors in my limbs betraying my unease.

"That's OK," Fred reassured me, casting a sympathetic glance in my direction. "Have you been up there long?"

I nodded.

"I'm sure they miss you," Fred offered.

It wasn't until I took another step downwards that his comment registered fully. "They? Who?"

"Oh. You know. Your family. Your friends," Fred replied vaguely.

"Do you think so?"

Fred didn't answer, but I was already too preoccupied with the unexpected sight of daylight filtering through the kitchen window, causing me to pause on the last step and squint against the brightness.

"Come on, one more and we're there," Fred urged, his hand still gripping my left arm firmly.

"It's daylight," I exclaimed, the realization dawning on me as I glanced around at the surroundings.

"Yeah," Fred confirmed casually.

"What time is it?"

"Oh. About five, I'd say. Come on," Fred urged me onward, but I remained rooted to the spot, my mind spinning with confusion.

Perplexed, I stood there, stunned by the penetrating daylight that seemed to defy the logic of the situation. *Did time go back? No. It only does that when I'm up in that room,* I reminded myself.

"Come on. One more," Fred repeated, breaking me out of my reverie, his voice gentle but insistent.

With a deep breath, I mustered the resolve to take the final step. Fred swung open the door, flooding the doorway with a bright light that temporarily impeded my vision. Shielding my eyes with my hand, I eventually adjusted to the glare.

"Oh, my God," I exclaimed, squinting against the sunlight. "It's like . . . it's like summer out."

"It *is* summer," Fred chirped cheerfully, a faint smile playing on his lips. "Sit on the steps for a minute while I grab your bike."

"My bike?" I echoed, watching as Fred laboriously picked up the mountain bike from the gravel and walked it over to me. Taking a seat on the steps, I couldn't help but marvel at the sight of my bare legs, now youthful and unblemished. The revelation was overwhelming, prompting me to stand once again.

"I'm... I'm in my... I'm in my cycling clothes," I stammered, running my hands along the silky fabric of my cycling shirt. "I'm... I'm me! My voice. I have my voice again."

"You feeling better?" Fred inquired, his gaze shifting to my shoulders. "You've got some blood on ya. You hit your head or somethin'?"

I furrowed my brow in confusion, reaching around to feel the dried blood on the goose egg-sized bump. "Ow! That hurts," I winced, the pain bringing back a flood of memories. "Oh yeah. Yeah. I remember, now," I said, a faint grin forming on my lips as the pieces of the puzzle fell into place.

"Come on," Fred urged, pushing the bike along with him. "I'll walk your bike home for you." He paused, glancing back at me. "You comin'?"

"Yes. Yes. I'm coming."

We continued along the dirt road, the crunch of gravel beneath our feet echoing in the quiet afternoon. As we reached the end of the road, I looked up to see the weathered sign that simply read "Host Road."

The End

Manufactured by Amazon.ca
Bolton, ON